BLEEDING SOULS SAVED BY LOVE

Spinning Gold:

Wicked Warriors MC

Utah Chapter

A Rumpelstiltskin Retelling

SOFIA AVES

Contents

Blurb

Nameless. Scarred. Broken. Nadir is intimate with the darkest corners of his soul.

Even a ruined man has a heart.

Kade Ryan understands everything about hitting rock bottom. Known as Nadir inside his local Utah MC chapter, Kade has little information of where he came from and who his family is meant to be.

During a raid to rescue women snatched from their homes by a rival club that deal with sex-trafficking, he discovers an abandoned infant. Reminded of his own history and unable to leave the child, Kade takes the baby to the only woman he trusts—his foster mother.

The abandoned infant isn't the sole person of interest. Summer Holmes stands out amongst the rescued women from the rival club. More than out of place, Nadir is drawn to her, and claims her as his own despite the mistrust of his MC brothers.

But Summer knows something about Nadir that no one else does. She knows his name...

SPINNING GOLD is a standalone MC dark romance retelling of Rumpelstiltskin.

A fairytale is a door to your darkest dreams.

Trigger Warning

SPINNING GOLD is a MC Club dark romance retelling of Rumpelstiltskin's legend.

It includes recounting of sexually abusive situations and dark themes.

SPINNING GOLD may not be suitable for all readers.

Chapter One

Nadir

"Ready to raise hell, boys?" Zenith twisted his wrist. The wicked blade in his palm glinted beneath the streetlights.

Murmurs of agreement followed his call to action, my own amongst them. He shared a shadowed look with me, and I nodded.

"You have your jobs. Do them cleanly and get the fuck out. Don't hang around to air grievances. We're not the fucking Sunday lunch ladies."

Soft laughter filled the air.

I stared across the road at the building that seemed far too quiet for a Friday night. The St. George Dragon's clubhouse didn't sport a single light, though the strip club that ran out of the back of the place should have been running at full tilt.

The parking lot was empty.

"Maybe they aren't home?" Tim, a skerrick over twenty years old and green as hell, offered. A hopeful edge to his voice drove my simmering rage higher.

"This isn't a church picnic, Prospect!" I barked, releasing the rein to my fury the slightest degree.

The group of men surrounding me quietened, and the prospect ducked his head.

"Sorry, sir."

Rambo clapped the back of his head. "Boy, we need to have a talk when we all get back."

"Yes—" The prospect earned himself a rough slap on the back before dropping any more *sirs* to his sire.

"All right. Don't dawdle, be efficient, and then we can get back to our regular program. All right, ladies?"

A few murmurs filled the small alleyway between two industrial buildings the twenty-odd of us currently occupied. It was far too small for men who shouldn't ever have been stuffed into close confines, but it gave us a solid vantage point despite the overpowering mix of stale piss and body odor. If anyone looked down the bottleneck, our leather cuts jammed between cement walls like sardines would have stood out.

But no one came by. Not a soul, a stray dog, or a drunk wobbling his way to the next pisspot.

I half expected a tumbleweed to roll across the grit-scattered road.

An outsider to the club might have expected us to charge straight across the street, but we weren't that stupid. No one would drive down this road tonight or take a stroll through the industrial area. We closed the roads before nightfall, positioning prospects at either end to deter any random who might end up in the middle of a turf-based bloodbath.

The car park had already been empty when we arrived, which gave me no small degree of tension. Pushing my clenched gut aside, I focused on the job at hand. Fear had no place. I could fall apart like a bitch when it was all over, and I had a beer in my hand back at the clubhouse.

Each member peeled off, returning around the back of the buildings that surrounded us. Every man had his assignment, and I had no doubt they would do it well.

"We go in, clean the place out of Dragons, and get the fuck out," Zenith murmured at my side.

"They're good, Pres. We've planned it out well."

"Always something at the other end that fucks it all up."

I nodded in silent agreement. The last time we had been in a turf war with another club, things hadn't turned out so well on either side. Now, the Wicked Warriors had as many prospects filling our ranks as we did established and loyal members. I had hope for the boys working their way up. There was some good blood there, and I'd stepped in to train them myself.

Assuming we all made it through the night.

"You ready?" I asked softly, never taking my eyes off the building across the road.

Zenith jerked his head in a quick nod. "Let's get this done. My cock's aching for some pretty pussy."

Together, we alone stepped out from between the buildings, staying to the shadows. It was a risky move; if they had gunmen inside and were aware of our presence, we could be riddled with bullets within seconds. But our intel was solid, and we crossed the road unimpeded.

"Too fucking quiet," Zenith growled. His narrowed gaze flicked across the open carpark.

I nodded, my teeth grinding. Pain shot through my jaw. I took that paltry offering and used it, kicking in the front door to the rival club's base.

Inside, the bar was full of bodies, but they weren't the ones we expected.

"What the fuck is going on here?" Zenith growled at my side.

I stepped into the main room as my boys entered through side and back doors, their weapons aimed, gazes focused. One by one they shook their heads. I made a quick hand movement, sending four of them back out the doors they'd entered through to investigate what hellish sort of cluster fuck we had walked into.

Exchanging a hard look with Zenith, I knelt beside the closest body, turning it over with caution. Her. A woman's hands were bound behind her back, so tight her swollen fingers were suffused with purple. Dirty blonde hair tangled in a mess that hung over her shoulders in a white-gold halo, the shade brighter than my own shoulder-length blond hair.

She groaned as I rolled her, heavy lashes fluttering open to catch me in a brilliant aquamarine gaze that took me instantly to a beach somewhere in the world that I'd seen only in a magazine. A piece of cloth was stuffed into her mouth, tied over with another to gag her.

Tears tracked her cheeks, though she stared up at me, frozen, and I recognized her glazed look. *Terror.* Anything unknown. Fear and I had a long-term relationship that I refused to let define me, and I'd do anything in that moment to take that same understanding of what lay in the shadows from her stunning eyes.

I tugged the gag down, careful not to scrape her face with my nails, my handgun lowered to my side. Her gaze flicked to it, then back to my face. She stared at me and slicked dry lips with a pink tongue. Grazes covered her face, bruises bloomed over her cheeks. I brushed my thumb over one, wanting to cradle her into my arms, tell her she was safe and that the assholes who had hurt her would never be able to ever again.

She flinched when Zenith knelt to slice through her bonds, but he was onto the next girl before she could turn enough to look at him.

"What happened here?" I asked softly, drawing her attention back to me. I didn't want to startle her, but with over a dozen women littering the clubhouse floor and my boys standing around with no idea what to do, I needed information.

And we needed to get the fuck out.

The wrongness of the place hung over the abandoned clubhouse in a shroud. Urgency replaced the clench in my gut.

She stared at me with those aqua eyes, and I lost myself in her again. When I finally snapped out of my reverie, she'd started talking.

"...have been taking girls and forcing them to work in the rooms above the strip club." She winced as she gestured to a door at the back of the dingy room that presumably led to the strip club beyond.

My stomach tightened as I took in her words.

"Are you saying the Dragons trafficked women into the sex trade? Forced?" Rage built in me, a dark swarm of vengeance for the women who littered the floor like so many discarded toys until my only option was to tear the cesspool apart and seek their revenge on any living soul I could find.

Sure, the Wicked Warriors had plenty of our own club bunnies and a strip club but not one woman was forced to work, and we paid damn well.

She held my gaze. Though I knew my fury must have been terrifying, I didn't bother to keep it off my face.

"Yes," she rasped, running her fingers over her wrists. Deep indents and tears rent her skin in wounds that would take weeks to heal, if she didn't scar.

I caught her wrists in my hands, massaging the marks with care to encourage her circulation, but not damage her any further. Her cold hands grew warmer in mine as I rubbed them, and though the pins and needles sensation must have been excruciating, she never complained, just held my gaze with those fearful eyes.

When I spoke again, my words came out tight, through a constricted throat. "Did they force you?"

Her soft lips pressed together, and she gave me a single jerk of her head. Dirty blonde curls fluttered around her face, and a new emotion filled her ocean-blue gaze. *Shame.*

Those fucking bastards.

I gathered her into my arms, needing to hold her, feel her softness against my body before the rage that brewed deep within me tore loose and obliterated everything in its path.

We'd known there were issues with the Dragons intercepting our last weapons delivery, and no one likes a poacher on their turf. The rival club had a bad rep for being rough with their girls in the club. Hell...we all had some interests in that area.

The Pres had a sadistic streak, but he made certain every girl he hurt shared his craving for painsluts and enjoyed it—in advance—and he cared for them afterward.

But taking women from their homes, stealing their lives away to shove them into our world? It took a special kind of evil to delve so low. The kind of evil I was prepared to wipe from the surface of my city.

"Need you, Nadir. Prospects will take the women back to the clubhouse." Zenith spoke quietly at my side, his voice heavy with emotion the control freak never allowed to compromise his objectivity.

I expected the harem that the boys had been cleaned up to squawk at this, to fight for their freedom.

Silence filled the clubhouse, broken by prospects scuffing their shoes in the wake of a broken raid.

Zenith and I exchanged a glance. Either the girls were plants and happy, hardened sex workers, or they were too terrified out of their fucking minds to make a sound, even in the face of a rescue. Maybe so bad they didn't recognize the rescue in progress.

I nodded and looked down at the woman I cradled in my arms. "What's your name, babe?"

"Summer," she croaked.

How fucking apt.

Movement shifted in my peripherals. I grabbed the nearest prospect with one hand, wondering what in the hell I was doing, but I didn't have time to second guess myself. What was his damn name? Lennard? Skinnard? *Fuck it.* The kid was getting a name, and I prayed it was the right one.

I stared into those azure eyes that shifted to the slightest hint of green. "Summer. Lenny here is going to take you back to the clubhouse. Ours. You'll be safe there. Get something to eat, get yourself clean. He'll take you to my room. Use my clothes. I'll buy you more. No one will touch you. Right, Prospect?"

"Right!" Lenny stammered.

I held her tight, watching for her consent before I sent her anywhere. Too much had been taken from these girls, and now was as good a time as any for them to have some minute aspect of control over their own destinies.

She jerked her head with a gasp. I brushed my fingers over her full lips. Her eyes flared wide, and I set her on her feet so I knew she would be all right walking away from me for now.

Back the fuck off, junior. She's traumatized.

Not one of the prospects or club members had better touch her before I got back. A protective urge swept over me, though I buried it deep in the knowledge that these women had been stolen from their homes. That some of them might not have a place to go back to.

Like me.

Most of my attention was focused on Summer. I tucked my key into the pocket of her jeans, squeezing her hands when she tried to protest. "I'm not taking advantage of you, babe. I just want you safe while I'm not there to do it myself." I sent her a lopsided grin, squeezing her icy hand again when she murmured something in her cracked voice.

Whatever it was, it could be dealt with when I got back to the clubhouse.

Zenith shot me a closed look over his shoulder as he organized the girls into pairs and filed them out the door under Deimos' protection. They would be fine, though my gut roiled at the obvious setup we'd walked into. It could have been a hell of mess and gunfire, but we were walking out with their prized possessions unscathed. Why?

The unanswered question irritated me. *Not knowing* was a personal hang-up I'd dragged along as baggage from my earliest years.

"What are you doing, Nadir?" Zenith's faint accent broke through his own concern, though I knew he'd likely only show it to me or his family. To everyone else, he was the impenetrable boulder we weathered ourselves on, trying to match his standard before we broke.

"Have we found the cache?" I didn't look at him. His question was something else that could wait until we got home.

Zenith pointed at me and backed up to the door at the rear of the room. "We'll talk later," he promised.

I grumbled under my breath, following him into the strip club and the rooms beyond. While Zenith and a few of the patched members circuited the floor, pulling the bar apart, I took the stairs two at a time to search the rooms above.

Some were set out in fantasy themes, or historical settings. Costumes hung from draperies that artfully disguised peeling paint. Other rooms looked like they had been lived in for some time. Clothes littered the floor, and bedding was a rumpled and soiled mess. The shared bathroom was no better, and the whole place stank of stale piss, sex, and fear.

I cleared the final room and having found fuck all evidence the Dragons had taken the weapons, I turned back down the hall. My irritation transformed me into a seriously testy man. The next person I came across was likely to earn himself a beating if I didn't get some answers to the questions that swirled nauseatingly in my mind.

Where are the weapons?

Have we been set up?

Who the fuck are the women and where did they come from?

Why hadn't we heard about the trafficking? Gritting my teeth, I slipped my gun back into its holster and headed for the stairs.

A cry stopped me in my tracks.

A *baby's* cry.

Chapter Two

Nadir

I blinked, pivoted on my heel, and waited.

The cry was muffled, but it was there, as though a barrier separated us. I strode the length of the hall to the rear wall and punched through it.

The exertion felt good.

Breaking the false wall felt better.

Plaster rained down on me. I pushed the dusty pieces aside and pulled open the door that had shifted with my blow.

Inside was a normal-looking office, albeit a messy one, filled with a desk and chairs. Paperwork scattered the desktop. A club pennant hung across one wall next to a row of faded, black and white framed photographs. What sat so out of place in the obvious business environment was the baby in a cradle in the far corner of the room. The child squalled quietly, rubbing his tiny, smushed face piteously along his mattress as though searching for something.

I crossed the room, keeping a wary eye on the door. The baby, a boy I assumed for all the blue sheets and the sleeping bag that covered his miniature, fragile body, reached up a plump hand to me.

"Hey, buddy," I murmured, extracting my gun.

Reaching out with my free hand, I nudged his plump palm, and his fingers closed around mine in a reflex action. He couldn't be more than six months old at a stretch. Surely he belonged to one of the members and hadn't been abandoned in their exodus. I swore under my breath and hoped to hell that a suspicion growing in my chest was wrong.

Disengaging my hand, I risked a glance at the little guy, still covering the door. "I'll be right back, little man. Promise."

I opened the office door—the real one—and poked my head around it briefly. The hallway beyond was clear. Sidling out the door and along the wall, I checked every room, but the top floor of the building adjoining the strip club was as deserted as the Dragon's clubhouse. Gritting my teeth, I checked the bottom floor as well, and discovered two things.

First, that it was empty.

Second, they had all our guns.

I didn't dare to touch the cache of weapons piled high on a billiard table in the center of the room. Every moment it felt more like a setup, and the empty place gave me the creeps. A quick check at the streetscape beyond confirmed the abandoned feeling. The building, the guns. The baby.

Leaning my back to a wall where I could see every door and window, plus the stairs, I sent off a short message to Zenith.

His reply was instant and mirrored my own.

Get the fuck out of there, fucktard.

Well, close enough. I took the stairs at a run, halting in the office only to gather a small, wiggly bundle in my arms, and headed back to Zenith.

"The fuck is that, Nadir?" he thundered. "We don't steal kids."

"He was abandoned in the office. I'll take him to Maria's place. He'll be safe there until I can figure out what to do."

Zenith regarded me with a mixed air of amusement and exasperation. "Your past catching up with you?"

"Probably. See you in an hour or so."

"Not to see me. You want that pretty pussy you've stuffed in your room." He laughed, motioning everyone else out.

I gritted my teeth and headed back to my truck where I'd parked in a side street, in the event we needed to tote the reclaimed weapons back home. Damn lucky, as a baby on a bike was a terrible fucking idea.

Bundling the tiny boy in my jacket, I strapped him into the passenger seat as best I could, making a lopsided nest of my jacket, and barricaded him in with my riding boots on either side.

I placed my hand lightly on the little guy's chest and put the truck into gear with my other hand. It would be an interesting drive across town. Maria's home was only fifteen minutes away, and the late hour meant little traffic.

He never made a sound all the way across town and by the time I reached the house, I was certain he had fallen asleep, lulled by the purr of the engine and noise of the tires.

I pulled up out the front, and by the time I had detangled his impromptu bedding, Maria was at my door, taking him from me.

"Little man," she cooed in a thickly accented voice that gave me visions of the only home I could remember. She tore her gaze from the baby. "What have you brought me, Kade? Tell me you didn't get a girl in trouble, eh?"

The name she had given me when I didn't know my own tumbled from her lips with familiarity as she peered into the cab of my truck as though looking for a random female that I'd not only managed to hide from her, but had knocked up and delivered a baby with zero mess.

"He's abandoned, Mama. I couldn't leave him there alone. I don't think he's in the system, and I'll do some investigating. Can you help me?" My plea was desperate, and pathetic. I wasn't sure how much was for the baby, and how much was for me.

My foster mother stared at me for a long moment before her face broke into her broad, trademark smile. "I would move the world for my Kade, but for you," she snuggled the baby to her bosom, "I will do anything." Maria looked up at me. "I have a girl with a newborn. We will share the load, and I have formula. I will not say a word." She smiled again, but a line creased her forehead, so out of place in her always smiling, rounded face.

"*Gracias.* I miss you." I hugged both her and the baby. The little guy shifted in his sleep. "I have to go to the clubhouse, but I'll come by first thing tomorrow. Send me a list of everything you need and I'll pick it up."

Mama nodded and freed one hand to pat my cheek. "Be good, Kade."

"Never." I gave her a cheeky grin and winked.

After one last, long look at the baby, I headed back to my truck. He was safe with her. Mama had raised more than thirty foster children in her lifetime, some legal and some who would never exist on paper. He would be cared for while I worked out where he belonged, if he had family left at all.

"Kade!" She called me back. I turned, my hand already on the door. "What is his name?"

I stared at her for a long moment, and yanked the door open with enough pent-up energy to twist my shoulder. My teeth ground together. Pain shot along my cheek, but this time there was no way to use it.

"I don't know."

Chapter Three

Summer

I sat inside someone else's room, staring at the closed door that didn't have a lock, and willed myself not to cry. Not that I'd had a room of my own or even a place to call home since Chester was born. My heart ached at the mere thought of him. Where was he? Was he safe?

I'd spent weeks creating the idea of a family around him, and now...he was gone. Surely they wouldn't hurt a baby. The inhumane thought tore a wounded animal sound from the back of my throat. I clamped my lips shut to prevent it from releasing further into the world. If I started screaming, I might never stop.

My mind calmed with the lack of oxygen I forced on it. No. These men were still that—men. Some of them had to have a family. Someone had to have a heart. While my brain whispered it was a fallacy, my heart clung to the thought in a tug-o-war destined to rip me apart in a silent battle.

Tears prickled at the corners of my eyes. I held the impending deluge at bay the same way I had for the past weeks and returned to staring at the door. A different door, but still a barrier between me and freedom. A ruckus traveled along the corridor in a muted cacophony from the bar downstairs we had been brought through when we arrived.

My mind flicked back to the girls I had been herded out of the St George Dragon's complex with which was more a dingy strip club with an even seedier bar attached—a bar where anything went except for personal hygiene or manners.

Were those girls downstairs now, being passed from man to man? Someone had mentioned something about bleeding souls, but I doubted any club could be that much different from another.

Maybe we had been the sacrificial offering on a turf war? The thought of the girls and I being passed around until we were less than useless, haggard or drug or alcohol-addicted sent a wave of nausea rising from the pit of my stomach.

But the men who had brought us in had been surprisingly gentle and as muted as the music and chatter from downstairs. Outside it, I could think in my tiny, impersonal bubble. A secondary glance around the room confirmed it held only a few pairs of jeans and leather biker jackets hanging in a closet with no door.

Beside the bed stood a small night table. A glass of water sat next to a well-thumbed bible and a hairbrush. The two items seemed at odds in such a place, considering the matte black and very lethal-looking handgun he had held. The man who had spoken to me. He had long, golden hair any woman would have been jealous of, which explained the brush. Two thick leather belts were slung over a scarred dresser that had its mirror removed. A single clay turtle sat on its pitted surface.

The face of the man who had spoken to me—the *only* man who had spoken to me as my young escort had been too terrified to open his mouth—obliterated the rest of the room.

Unshaven and filthy looking, like the rest of his brethren, he had talked to me on an almost human level. It had been enough to bring me out of the fog surrounding me, dulling each slap or poke to my meatless frame. Each leather-bound kiss to my skin.

I jammed the thoughts deep and returned to my assessment of my not-so-shining knight.

His touch had been gentle, even...respectful. And his eyes, like liquid caramel highlighted with golden slices, promised safety and threatened violence all in one glimpse. I curled on the bed in my soiled black tights, but had swapped out my tattered tee for the clean one offered. That had been a mistake. Now, the man's scent filled the air around me and stained my skin.

There went my head, romanticizing a savior who was as likely to rape me as rescue me. Proof I was utterly insane and that my captivity had broken me, and I hadn't noticed.

I let out a long clean breath that betrayed me in every capacity by shuddering at the end. Not even my body was under my control. Fucking brilliant. I gave a mental eye roll; my parents would have a field day with my language.

A mad grin broke out across my face that died a speedy and excruciating death. I'd never be welcome back with my parents, and I had no home. Their abandonment stung the worst. Nausea repeated on itself in my stomach until I hunched over numbed legs, folded beneath me for far too long on a bed that wasn't mine.

My forehead brushed the quilt, tattered and ragged at the edges, though it was the sort a grandmotherly type had made. Yet another out of place item in this contradictory man's room. His scent—leather and spice and diesel—filled my senses, leaving me heady with it. After too many nights of stale piss and pungent body odor, it seemed almost...pleasant.

I slammed my hands against the threadbare quilt that had seen too many nights. The bed's plush surface gave way just enough for the gesture to be unsatisfying. Discomfort fueled me from my mind fog. I pushed off from the bed, forcing my legs to work as circulation returned to unfeeling limbs. The pain was a welcome distraction.

Focused on that, I stumbled to the door, my arm outstretched. Being cooped up, without knowing my fate and the girls' fate was too much. After everything, fears ran around my head—I shook it and was rewarded with an instant headache. There was no point in narrowing my life down to which fear would be realized next. Hell, no. I would meet the next one head-on.

I grabbed the door handle and took a fortifying breath.

The scratched metal turned under my hand, though I made no move to twist it, and the door imploded inward. A warm body followed it. A very warm, *huge* body, topped with a swath of shoulder-length, golden hair and eyes I could never have forgotten and likely never would, their twin liquid embers burning pinpoints through my soul.

I backed up by reflex enough to accommodate his frame and stalled. Torn between retreating to the back of the room and edging past him, my body did the worst thing possible and betrayed me a second time. I froze on the spot, inches from his very bare chest beneath an open, embroidered leather vest.

Relief that I was in the right room, the one I had been directed to back in the Dragon's hellhole, washed over me followed hot on its heels by a cynical voice that whispered a single word.

Victim.

And that was something I would never be, ever again.

His hooded amber gaze swept over me, taking in my measure and worth in a single glance. The air stilled between us, the flurry of movement in the moment before already a faded memory. He turned his head to speak to someone behind him. Soft chatter reached my ears, but that wasn't what drew my attention. His body still blocked the doorway. Hard lines, tattoos, and scars covered only lean, ripped muscle.

That fact alone made him terrifying and formidable in a single glance, but also strangely beautiful. I gave him the same once over he had given me, taking in the low-slung black riding leathers, well-worn by the creases, and the heavy silver belt buckle. But the lack of anything fluffy on this man—the term itself was laughable—gave him a brutally honest and unapologetic appearance. Something solid that I could trust.

I blinked and began to laugh. Not only was the situation ridiculous, but I was laughing in the face of a potentially murderous lunatic. And for that, I laughed all the harder. The tears that had prickled the corners of my eyes before ran anew, coating my cheeks in salt and pent-up sorrow.

The still-terrified face of the young man who had escorted me into this room in the first place stared at me over a mass of muscle and ink and was gone.

Then the man who owned those startling eyes turned back to face me, piercing me straight through.

My laughter ceased under his hard glare. He seemed to have only one intensity setting and it was running on high all the time.

Without a word, I knew two things. One, I was about to find out whether I was right in my assessment of his nature. Two, without saying a single word or taking another step, from the way his gaze flared and hooded all at once, that I was in a hell of a lot of trouble.

The door shut with a softened thud as it jammed in the doorframe. It registered loud enough to my frazzled nerves that I jumped.

"You're safe here." The giant's lips moved.

I blinked. Whatever demand or unspoken threat I might have expected to hear, it wasn't that. If I hadn't seen him say the words, I would have accused my brain of making them up.

"What?" *Eloquent, Summer.* Apparently, my recent state had ruined my survival skills altogether.

The giant gave me a ghost of a not-quite-there smile and eased around me. I pivoted as he passed, each of us moving in concert around the other, following, but not touching.

The door! No lock!

My brain screamed all the useful things to my unresponsive body.

25

"Summer?" He looked over his shoulder.

I concentrated my gaze on a point between his shoulder blades, tracing over the ink that wound its way from beneath his hair to where it disappeared into his jeans. A thorny vine crisscrossed over the valley between twin ridges of muscle. The longer I stared, the more I understood, making out individual characters until the whole thing ran around in my head.

"Nameless and unknown." I raised my head, finally meeting his terrifying gaze. The urge to clam up was strong, but not greater than my need to know I'd gotten it right. "But it just repeats, over and over...wait. The vine— it has no ending? Does it twist back on itself at the top and bottom?" I took a step closer, gesturing at his hair.

His eyes widened then narrowed, and I bore the full brunt of his intensity.

My body froze on the spot.

Prey.

Not the sort you send to God. The one that gets eaten.

His lips twitched as though he was going to say something, then stilled. After a moment of excruciating silence, he turned around to face me. "Would you like to check?" His hand grazed his silver belt buckle, rough-looking fingers tracing over the leather.

I swallowed and choked on my denial. "No!" I managed to shove the word out, though my eyes watered at its force.

He raised both eyebrows and reached for the glass of water on his bedside table. "Don't die on me," he murmured. The glass was pressed into my hand, though I tried to wave him away. "I usually get a lot further into a seduction than a single line before they pass out."

I'd managed to get a sip of water into my mouth without coughing it up and began to splutter anew. He observed me with something akin to amusement. I stared at him with accusing eyes while my brain whispered important things I ignored.

"You do what?" I choked out. "And you're not seducing me. I was just, uh—" *Reading your ink* sounded more or less like a pickup line. My head defogged along with my windpipe, and I had a moment of clarity. "I'm not a club bunny." The words came out without a stutter, unlike the first time I had said them. My cheeks flamed with embarrassment and shame at the memory.

Different place. Not here not here not here—

"Interesting reaction. But you could read my tattoo?" Up went the eyebrows again.

"I said as much." I clamped my mouth shut. Attitude only earned me bruises. I'd learned that far too slowly, naivety allowing me to believe that fighting was akin to survival.

"Not-a-club-bunny Summer—" he took a step in my direction, and I mirrored him in a silent farce that brought the wall to my back, "—that's written in Sanskrit. And you read it." He frowned down at me.

His arms braced against the wall on each side of my head, forming a cage of ink and muscle.

I pressed myself back against the wall, flattening as much as possible. Becoming insignificant next to him should have been an easy feat, but it proved impossible. I couldn't get away from him. Air evacuated from the diminished space between us. "So?"

He huffed a soft laugh that set nerves on fire all over my body. "How many people do you know who can read Sanskrit to start with and then when it's all twisted and stylized like that? Who are you, Summer?"

I stared up at him, trapped in the glare of those liquid eyes. "I— I don't know."

"That makes two of us." His face shuttered, but he didn't back away.

Pressure built in my chest. If I didn't manage to suck in air soon, I'd pass out.

"What's your name?" I blurted, using my last precious breath on something so frivolous.

"I thought you were smart, Summer." He leaned in, shrinking the pocket of air that formed no barrier at all between us. "Nameless and unknown, remember?"

"Well, yes, but—" I pressed my lips together. "What do people actually *call* you? And what am I doing here? Are the girls okay? Where's—"

"Nadir."

A single, soft word cut through my word vomit and silenced me.

Chapter Four

Nadir

"The bottomless? Rarity? No, that's not right either." Island blue eyes narrowed as she considered her words and their meaning. *Summer.* Pretty name for a pretty girl made all the more stunning for her smarts.

Someone who takes the time to think.

It was a distinct rarity in my world and certainly in my life. But still...she was about to reach her own conclusions, and I didn't want to see how close she came to my truth.

"Summer," I warned. My hands turned into fists against the wall, my knuckles digging into the plaster behind her head. I braced my forearms there instead and closed the space I'd retained as a safety until only a breath separated us.

Summer didn't notice. Her gaze focused elsewhere as she turned the thought over and over. "Unfree..." Her head snapped up, aqua flashing at me. "Unworthy. Rock bottom."

"Thanks for that assessment," I said dryly.

She blinked and seemed to realize how close we were. "Oh—" she flattened her palms to the wall, twisting her head this way and that.

Some perverse part of me loved torturing her, but the main reason I needed her was to get answers. The other women we had rescued were currently holed up in the closed dance studio that bordered on the strippers' apartments, and most of them couldn't put a sentence together, cowering whenever a man approached.

Donna, who ran the club under Zenith's eye, had taken them all in without question, offering food, showers, and clean clothes. Most of the women had responded to that, but a few hadn't, and I knew we had to get them the help they needed.

That same need drew on the eternal fire that supplied me with an endless source of darkness. We needed to find out why the women had been taken, and if there were any more that had gone missing. For once, I was almost inclined to involve cops. Like many clubs, we had a few pet ones of our own, but using them still rankled me.

Right now, my best source of information was pinned against my wall, all too soft and tempting looking. "Educated little thing, aren't you?"

"Well, yes, if I'd been allowed to continue study but"—her voice dropped to a whisper—"that avenue is closed to me, now."

"Why?"

"Why? Because what middle-class family wants a damaged girl back who they gave away to a crime syndicate as *payment*? The college would never allow me back or any of the girls. None of us can afford it. Lives lost, lives ruined." Bottled fury raged silently at me beneath her seething words.

It took me a moment to catch on, but once I had, I welcomed that blazing blue flame she offered. "How many lives lost, Summer?" Her mouth clamped shut, and her chin dropped. I curled my fingers beneath her chin and gently lifted her gaze back to me. She met me with resistance, but tiny and malnourished as she was, she had no hope of physically matching me.

Is that how you want to start with her?

Start what, exactly? The women were here for their safety. Once we figured out where their homes were and that they were safe, we'd send them right back to their homes unless they elected to stay, working under the club's protection. I wasn't keeping Summer, and I sure as hell wasn't getting involved with her.

Fucking liar.

I shoved the sentiment aside and refocused on my tasks. Zenith wanted answers, and if I didn't get them soon, he'd come looking. While I might have reservations, he'd have no trouble turning on the charm to get his way, and get her into his bed, heedless of the trauma she had suffered.

"How many, Summer?"

Her stunning gaze lifted to meet mine. "Just one. But she was the best of us all."

Tears welled and broke, cascading over gaunt cheeks, and took my heart right along with them.

"Fuck," I swore.

Add murder to the barrel, and someone—several someones—would be asking questions. The likelihood of cops not becoming involved at this point was reduced to less than zero.

Summer jerked as though I'd barked at her. I swallowed and leaned my forehead against hers, breaking the no-contact pretense we'd kept up since I'd entered the room.

She gasped but didn't twist away. The shock slowed the flow of her tears and slowly, they ceased.

"Who, honey? I need a name." *A full one, and not a fake or a made-up one.* But I didn't add that and let her take the time she needed to answer.

A teardrop clung to her long, black lashes. She swiped the remnants of her grief away with the backs of her hands, shattering the perfect pear-shaped jewel. "Amanda. She— she didn't have anyone. No— no family. Not anymore."

I frowned at her stutter, certain she had omitted something. "I'll remember that. Tell me what they were doing to the girls, Summer. Let me help them."

"No." Her face closed me off, and something new flared in her aquamarine gaze. Something that drew a different sort of ache from my heart and left my lips tingling.

Defiance.

Her show of strength gave me hope. Whatever ordeal the assholes had put her through, she would recover through pure will, and I admired her for it. But that meant I still didn't have the answers I needed to let her drop below Zenith's radar.

I sighed and shifted back so I could see her face in full. "I need more than that, babe. Tell me where they came from. I can make some calls and let them go home."

"No." She shook her head, her face ablaze with righteous anger.

"No? You don't want them to go home? What am I missing here?"

"Not that they don't want to, but that they have no home to go to. Amanda tried. And she— she—" The tears started again.

I closed my eyes and banged my fist gently against the wall above her head. The plaster reverberated at her back; I'd hit it harder than I had intended.

She jumped, cowering from the sound.

"Fucking hell." I wrapped my arms around her stiff form and pulled her to my chest without thinking it through. She stood rigid in my embrace as I pressed my chin to the top of her head. "Summer, I'm not going to hurt you. No one here is. You. Are. Safe."

"I'll never be safe." She shook her head, adamant, or stubborn, or both.

The corner of my mouth quirked. I was beginning to really like this girl, who bore her battle scars proud and refused to back down in the face of an uncertainty I knew I could never fathom.

I wound one arm around her back, holding her to me, and used my other hand to tilt her head back, brushing tears from her cheeks with my thumb. Her body softened at the tender, protective contact and I sent up a silent prayer in thanks to any angel who was having a shit enough day to be on my watch.

Trusting eyes stared up at me.

My heart clenched hard in an empty cavity. "I promi—"

The door to my room flung open hard enough to hit the wall behind it. Plaster flaked to the floor. Summer cowered in my arms, her body pressed to my chest. A shiver started in her shoulders that wracked her head to toe.

I held her tight to me, shielding her with my back half-turned to the barrage I knew to expect.

Zenith stood in the doorway, a beer clutched in one hand. "Fuck me. I've heard some stories, and I still haven't had time for pussy. She talked yet?"

My teeth clenched hard enough to grind on each other. I pried them apart, inhaling long breaths through my nose. "We were getting there. Privacy wouldn't fucking hurt."

"You've never wanted privacy before." Zenith snorted.

I twisted to glare at him over my shoulder. "Never had something to care about before." If I turned her over to the pres, no matter how loyal I was, she'd end up in his bed. No part of me could accept that now I'd had my arms around her, and there was no way in any of the seven hells I could let anyone else touch her, either. The thought flitted through my mind and took up residence and before I could think it through and weigh up the risk as I always did, I acted on it. "Summer's mine."

Zenith's eyes widened. He opened his mouth, but nothing came out.

I took advantage of the moment's reprieve to do something truly stupid.

Without finding out if she had been sexually assaulted or how the Dragons had abused her, I gripped her chin between firm fingers, bent my head, and kissed her.

Really fucking intimately kissed her.

Not a peck or a chaste, closed-mouth kiss. No half-hearted shit. I claimed her in a soul-deep kiss that seared her into my bloodstream and ruined me for anyone else, ever.

And she opened to me.

I didn't know if it was a natural reaction from her, if the moment of intimacy we shared had broken her down, or if she'd already been that way when I found her. Summer's lips parted beneath my onslaught, my kiss rough enough to bruise her tender skin, deep enough to send the need for her rocketing straight to my cock.

But it was greater than that. She hadn't run from me as I'd expected when I'd entered the room and turned my back to her. Instead, she'd stayed, and seen me, actually looked at me, and queried things no one had asked me for a long time.

Granted, I wasn't big on questions and had a violent as fuck reputation, but Summer had spoken to me as a person, though she didn't know me.

Now she has a lifelong chance to understand that.

The cynical little voice was back.

"The fuck." Zenith's disgusted voice broke over my head. "Fucking church when you come down, brother."

I didn't care. Nor did I stop kissing Summer until his footfalls left the upstairs hall altogether. When my door finally clicked shut of its own volition, I softened the kiss, grazing my lips across hers. Sensation ran down my spine, settling at its base in a low ache that heightened my need for her beneath me.

That would have to wait. I'd taken enough liberties in an attempt to save her, or maybe keep her for myself, and now she needed to have her own say.

I raised my head, breaking the kiss, and stared down at her.

Summer's head was tipped back, her lips swollen and flushed from our makeout session. Her eyes were half-closed, the lines on her face soft and dozy as she swayed into me.

Her cheek curved beneath my knuckles. I grazed them along her jaw and followed them with my lips.

Her eyelashes fluttered open, and she sucked in a great gulp of air. The fingers I found curled around my biceps tightened until her nails dug into my ink. I had no doubt there would be small scratches in the indents when I unpicked them from my skin.

"Summer. Babe," I murmured. Her flaxen hair draped over the arm I wound around her back. I curved a hand into it, cradling the back of her head to take the weight off her neck. "Hey. Tell me you're okay. I'm sorry. You have no idea what—"

Her palm cracked across my cheek and left my skin stinging in her wake. Her strength shocked me, more than the action I'd expected, anyway. But that she had enough power to put genuine force into the blow from the waif-like look of her...she was less than a slip of a girl, little more than a wraith.

Summer blinked at me, the dozy look lingering as those same fingers that had bruised my cheek pressed to her lips. Wonder and horror warred in her face. "Why?"

I balanced on a dangerous precipice, trying to play catch up as she switched from topic to topic in a disjointed manner and attempted to be non-threatening at the same time.

Magnificent fucking fail right there, my friend.

"If you need to slap me again, do it, girl. Whatever you need." I hadn't asked her, and I'd been no better than the assholes I'd taken her from, but by God, I'd try to fix it first. "Whatever you need," I repeated a little more slowly this time.

"No." She shook her head. "Why did you kiss me?"

"Because I don't want anyone else touching you."

She nodded and seemed to accept that. A small crease dipped between her brows. "And he would have touched me?"

"Pres? He might have tried to come off as a good guy, and he is. Well, no, that's an outright lie. He's mostly good. We all are, to an extent but—" *Fuck me.* Could I ramble on any longer? "The point is that you would have ended up in his bed and I didn't want that," I finished softly.

Ocean deep eyes considered me. "And being in yours is better than being passed around?" Her voice trembled on the last two words, but her defiance returned, blazing at me in full force.

"What? No. No, we're not like that."

"Then why do I need you?"

I stared at her, and my mouth dropped half-open. For the first time, I had no nice words or even anything snarky to throw back in banter. My brain remained silent and blank in the face of her clarity.

I cleared my throat. "Nothing. No reason at all."

"So, if I wanted to walk out of here, right now, I could, and no one would stop me or hurt me?"

My throat burned with the answer I was about to give her.

"Yes. Though I'd prefer—"

"Then I need to go."

My arms dropped to my sides.

Summer backed away, a step at a time, her bare feet making no sound on my filthy floorboards, and pulled my lockless door open.

Chapter Five

Summer

"**No.**"

For the second time in seemingly as many minutes, the dark-haired behemoth stood in the doorway of Nadir's room, glowering at me. He was the opposite of Nadir in all things; bulky, where Nadir was lean, ripped muscle, dark and short-haired versus long, golden locks.

The problem was that this time, two walls of pure muscle sandwiched me. I'd never considered myself claustrophobic, but right now, I'd opt in, or out, as it were. I took a step backward and butted into Nadir.

His hand closed around my waist, holding me against his hard frame. "What part of privacy are you not getting here, Pres?"

Pres. I filed the unfamiliar term away in my collection, creating a world in my head around Nadir.

Run run run—

But my legs stayed grounded, though they were somewhat wobbly after his life-altering kiss. Rather than risking a suicidal dash past Nadir's boss I stayed put and leaned into his touch. Essentially, I'd exchanged one captor for another. My rational, educated mind screamed Stockholm syndrome had been proven a myth, and my heart craved some sense of security. Apparently, I was so desperate to be loved and wanted that I would take the first thing offered.

But oh, what an offering.

"Get a door that locks, then." The big man rolled his eyes at Nadir.

They spoke over my head like I wasn't even there, carrying on their conversation while I shrank, an unused toy stuck between two big men. Unfortunately, the space seemed to shrink with me. I plummeted back into the land of hands poking and pulling at my skin and clothes, groping and—

An inhuman wail broke from my lips, and my hands hit the leather-covered chest in front of me in a slap that left my palms stinging.

My action achieved absolutely nothing except absolute silence and the attention of both men.

"Air," I gasped, all fish out of water. If this was to be my demise, then I was going out with no style whatsoever. The thought triggered my hysterics again. I'd definitely been born in the wrong century. Next, I'd be swooning at their feet.

I lashed out again, trying to free up space as my world grayed at the edges.

Hands touching poking prodding feeling under my clothes under my skin—

Cold air kissed my back. My cage disappeared, and I stumbled over my own feet in a failed attempt to seek balance. Weeks of uncertainty swirled in my head in an epic mind-crash as gravity wrapped her arms around me.

Warm hands closed on my shoulders, prying me out of the tiny ball I'd become, crouched on the grit-laden floor. I stared at individual specks, made out splinters working themselves free between the boards. A single point of focus, grounding me.

Until he spoke and ruined my serene bubble where I didn't have to worry about anything else in the world.

"Summer. Summer," he urged. Large hands squeezed my shoulders, and a familiar knuckle crooked beneath my chin.

I let him raise my gaze to meet his turbulent one.

Nadir stared at me, his brow dipped, though his lips twisted in the hint of a sardonic smile. "Took things too fast, huh?" He brushed my hair back from my face. "You need a safe place to sleep and heal, and I have that for you. I'm taking her to Mama's place." This last he spoke over his shoulder, twisted away from me.

"Not until I get my answers."

"Fuck you. They can wait, Zenith."

"No, they can't."

The pair bickered on like school kids, or maybe a married couple with decades of history. Which might have been interesting but—

"Did you mention the possibility of a shower? A real, clean one?" I whispered. My cheeks flamed as two piercing sets of eyes redirected my way. Once again, I was the center of their combined attention, and it was far too much to bear on top of everything else. My mind just didn't have sufficient capacity to process the additional sensory stimulation.

"You haven't had a shower in a while, huh?"

"Not a hot one, or without rust in it." I pressed wobbling lips together. I would not cry, I would *not*. Not again.

"I can promise you the best shower you've ever had," Nadir murmured.

There were no greater seductive words anyone could have said in that moment. I raised my gaze to lock with his as he wrapped broad arms around me. Not in a cage, exactly. He created an intimate space between us, around us. For the first time in an age, I was...safe. The thought seemed alien. I frowned, contemplating it. Though I knew what the word meant, I couldn't fathom how it applied to me.

"What is it?"

I smiled. He hadn't asked what was wrong; it would have been easier to ask what was right. That wasn't much, except for him. "I— you— I'm safe. Maybe. I think?" I tilted my head to one side, still trying to work it through.

The emotion that washed through his eyes, darkening them in an instant, floored me.

"I'll fucking kill them all," he growled. The sound reverberated from deep in his chest, primal, with the promise of violence.

Like his kiss, sweet and searching and dangerous all at once. A bottomless pit yawned in front of me, and I wasn't sure if I wanted to step over it, or into it.

"It's okay. You don't have to do that." *Not for me. I don't deserve your kindness.*

"I fucking well will. For you and for the others."

The thought of someone committing murder on my behalf grazed over my little bubble, not half as disturbing as it should have been. Nadir offered comfort, albeit a dark and dangerous sort, and I so desperately needed to take it.

"Ahem." A pointed cough came from the doorway. "When you're finished with your romantic floor picnic, get into my office. *Both* of you."

Nadir didn't turn away from me, but his eyes closed. His warmth was lost to me when he shuttered his gaze, and when he opened his eyes there was something raw reflected in their depths that I couldn't decipher. "Yes, Pres."

His hands flexed around my shoulders once. Nadir drew me up to standing, and by the time my shaking legs were strong beneath me, his bedroom doorway stood empty again. He led me to the door, and I padded along behind him, my fingers were wound in his, though I didn't remember doing it.

At the threshold, I hesitated. A thought niggled at my mind, something Zenith had said. The name suited him, for the mountain of a man. But it was his words that triggered me. "You go to church? Like, all of you?"

Besides that it wasn't Sunday yet, I couldn't imagine each grimy man seated at the bar downstairs genuflecting at a church or taking holy sacrament. Some clubs might be Christian-based, or so I assumed, knowing little of MC club culture. But the violence in these men's souls called to a different level of sinners. *Aren't we all?* I closed a door on my memories and refocused, recalling the worn bible on Nadir's bedside table.

His chest rumbled, and he barked a laugh that echoed along the corridor. "Church is another word for club meeting. My brothers have to attend if Pres calls for it, and so do I."

I frowned. "You're like a committee, then?"

Nadir's laughter filled the top story of the building. "My God, Summer. You'll be the death of me. We probably are—hell, we can bitch and dance around truths we don't want to face with the best of them. But for fuck's sake, don't let Zenith hear you say that."

"Noted." I flexed my fingers around his as he tugged on my hand. A question rose in his eyes when my feet didn't move, but my mind had started churning away after its enforced hiatus, processing at speed and I couldn't stop the flow of questions. "What about the bible on your night table?"

Nadir stilled. His gaze hooded, he turned his face away from me. "When you don't know where you come from or who you are, you seek answers wherever you think you'll find ones that matter." He strode forward, pulling me along with him.

I trotted to keep up, unable to match his long stride. Even that was coated in violence, or the threat of it. "Did you find any? Answers, that is?"

Nadir's hand clamped tight around mine. "Some of them."

And that was all he would say as he led me down the stairs to a door beside the long bar. The bar area was filled with men who looked similar to him, dressed in their leather vests. Each one sat silently, and every eye was fixed on where we were headed. The door to a small office stood ajar. I swallowed hard, unable to walk into a room that might seal my fate more firmly than it had months before, in a similar room, in a different clubhouse.

Nadir's hand pressed firmly between my shoulder blades and propelled me through to the other side.

I sat in a hard-backed chair that straightened my spine more than it wanted to after weeks of sleeping on a rug on the floor next to a dozen other women. Despite Nadir's comment about church being a meeting, sitting before Zenith in his throne-like gaming chair resembled nothing more than being dragged before the clergy to confess my sins.

I suspected he would be a hard taskmaster and my penance long if I stumbled.

Nadir stood behind me, his white-knuckled hands clasped to the back of my chair. I swallowed and tried to sit ramrod straight, but my muscles, already fatigued, protested. Spikes of pain radiated from my spine, and I sank back, my eyes closed. Warm hands clasped my shoulders, squeezing and massaging in a rhythm that left me groaning in relief of long abused and aching muscles.

"I'm not here for fucking porn noises." Zenith's disgusted voice reached me. "It's like you're here for marriage counseling and I hate digging into a man's private affairs," he grumbled.

My eyes flew open. A giggle escaped my lips, and I slammed my palm to cover them, but it was too late. I swallowed my horror at the slip.

Zenith sent me a rueful grin. "Good to see you smile, girl, and hear you laugh. Not the hysterical sort. Don't you pull any of that shit around me," he warned, but the smile stayed fixed on his face, transforming him into something a touch less menacing, and almost beautiful in a rugged, damaged sort of way.

I am safe.

I choked back the fear of understanding and craving security again. If it was torn away from me a second time, I wasn't sure I would survive to come out the other side the same.

You aren't the same though, are you? Daddy wouldn't like a ruined girl like you.

The thought of my family's betrayal brought tears to my eyes.

Zenith's brow dipped, and the humor faded from his face.

I stared up at the ceiling, blinking rapidly, but all that achieved was to trade one set of concerned eyes for another. I dropped my gaze and studied my hands twisted in my lap instead.

"Girl, I need—"

"Summer," Nadir interrupted.

I stared down at my fingers, twisting and turning like so many brittle worms in a roiling nest.

"Fine. Summer." Zenith paused.

The silence held until it was thick and unfathomable. I raised my head, willing myself not to cry. Or scream, or laugh at him, or do anything inappropriate. Control of my own body had deserted me, and I wasn't sure how much he was prepared to forgive, despite his open demeanor.

"Yes, Zenith." I straightened my spine the tiniest amount.

The corner of his mouth lifted. "Summer. I need you to tell me about the girls, about yourself. Where they have come from, and what's happened to them." He glanced over my head, communicating silently with Nadir. He jerked his chin, and his jaw set in a hard line. "If those girls can go home or they're from a long way away, then I have to let the police know. It's not my core function, but hell, I wouldn't want to keep wondering if my daughter was out there, if she was coming home or not."

"Do you have a daughter?" The words slipped out. I didn't try to pull them back. My mind wandered to Chester, but I had to focus. I could ask, soon.

"No." His gaze narrowed. "Do you?"

I shook my head. "But I—"

"Then tell me what I need to know, Summer." His voice took on a persuasive note, lulling me into a sense of security.

I hadn't realized I was leaning forward until Nadir squeezed my shoulder a little too hard, jerking me out of the trance Zenith induced. Nadir was right, his boss *was* dangerous. The sort of dangerous you didn't know had already happened to you until it was too late.

I leaned back into Nadir's embrace, and cleared my throat. "The girls don't want to go back. I don't know where they are from, where any are from, except for Amanda. It was our unspoken rule. Don't ask because it might jinx our chances of escaping." My throat clogged, and my stomach rose, battling for an exit strategy I wasn't willing to give. That rule had bonded us together in our isolation and our pain. Only one woman had broken it.

I pressed the back of my fist to my mouth and bit it, hard. The sharp pain overrode my nausea, and I breathed again.

A self-taught tactic I had learned on my road throughout purgatory.

"Come on, Summer. Were they from Utah, at least? Where were the Dragons drawing them from?"

"I— I don't know." I lied, and badly.

"Bullshit."

"I don't know."

"Fine." Zenith planted forearms the size of tree trunks—and not small ones—on his desk and loomed over them at me. Muscles popped in places

I didn't think muscles could exist. He bared his teeth. "Where are you from, Summer?"

I shrank back at his change of direction, taking the chair with me. My bare heels dug into the wooden floor, but Nadir trapped me in place with his body weight. I launched back and my head hit the wooden chair back. I twisted and curled onto my side—anything to get away from where this was heading.

"I can't go home."

"Why not? Because you think you're damaged? You're hurting. I get that." Zenith's gaze flicked up then back to me, though his tone softened. "But you will heal, and you have some of the best support and compassion standing right behind you."

"You calling me soft, Old Man?" Nadir hunched over, wrapping his arms around both me and my chair.

His embrace was no longer the cage I'd expected. My fingers curled around his wrists, unable to close completely. I inhaled his leather and spice scent and released a long breath that took up a whole lot of toxic, pent-up energy with it.

"I can't go home because my parents sold me to a minor mafia player who then passed me onto the Dragons when I was no longer...useful to him." I waited for the bitter tang, the wave of nausea to rise. When nothing happened, I took a cautious breath. "I have a high pain tolerance. Ex-high school athlete. I'm used to pushing myself and ignoring discomfort. Some of the men my ex passed me around to had...interesting tastes." I stopped short of saying unique because I'd found just how common violence toward women could be.

Zenith's brow darkened, a thunderstorm threatening to erupt. "Are you saying they hurt you?"

"Yes. In a way, I'm grateful for it. I was left alone in— in other respects. They tried different things with different girls. I became a pain bunny because I could zone out, distance from it. At first, they thought I liked it. Then it became a competition to see who could get a reaction from me."

"Stubborn, huh? Let me see," Zenith coaxed, half-rising from his seat.

I breathed again, and again my body gave no reaction. Numb, like the rest of me. *Finally*. I tilted my head back to hold Nadir's gaze and found him way too close. "You won't find me pretty after this." I pushed up and back. The chair slid soundlessly out from beneath me, and I stood on strong legs. The shaking was gone and by my own choice, not Zenith's seductive little coo, I gripped the sides of my top and half-turned, lifting it to bare my shoulders.

Twin gasps of horror filled the room. Nadir's turned into a hiss. His warmth hovered over my back, but never touched. "Fucking assholes. What sort of a man does this?"

"It's okay. They're healed. You can touch me without causing pain." *Now.*

"The sort that has no willpower, control, or respect for women." Zenith's hands closed over mine, exceedingly gentle for his magnitude. He tugged the material from my stiff fingers, drawing it over my back with infinite care. "Thank you for showing us, Summer. That took more balls than half my boys have." He kissed the top of my head. "You will describe these men for me in great detail. Where they were, what they did. You will relive this for me." He turned me to face him. "Because I will not allow another woman to suffer what you have. First, rest, and be clean. I will send you off with medical supplies. Nadir will get you any others you require."

"Mama has plenty. But something for infection would be handy."

"Done, brother. You have my blessing." Zenith's gaze caught and held mine. "While you're with Nadir, you have the club's protection. For what you have been through, you have mine for life."

A sob built in my throat, constricting my airway. The walls bent, the room swaying until everything reached me through a long-distant tunnel.

"You're beautiful. More so because you offered to show us your courage." Nadir's arms wrapped around me, tugging me out of Zenith's

56

office as I mouthed my thanks, unable to utter a single sound.

The bar area, so packed before, was almost deserted. Nadir spoke to a few men on the way out and grabbed the arm of a girl manning the bar. He whispered something in her ear. She nodded and disappeared out the back of the bar, reappearing a moment later with a matte black motorcycle helmet and a pair of black leather boots.

"It's all I had." She winked her apology at me. "But I think they'll fit."

"Thank you," I managed. My world blotted out for a moment as the helmet was pushed onto my head.

"Good fit?"

"I think so?" I offered, relieved my voice worked again. "I have no idea."

Nadir tested the helmet and made a sound in the back of his throat. "It's fine. Sit."

I sat, imagining I looked utterly ridiculous in a helmet indoors. Fingers caught my calf and traced over the stretchy material of my tights in a sure touch.

Nadir slid on one boot, then the other. They fit well, though I had never worn knee highs before. I rose, expecting to feel unsteady but I managed not to totter. The heel was chunky, and I gave the girl on the bar a wave and a muffled *thanks*.

Then I was outside. Nadir's hands closed around my waist, lifting me like I weighed nothing at all. He set me astride an enormous-looking bike, all back leather and chrome.

He sat in front of me, and I wrapped my arms tight around his waist. The engine roared to life, settling into a guttural roar that thrummed from my fingers to the tips of my toes.

"Hold on tight."

"Where are we going?" I called as Nadir peeled out of the parking lot.

"Home."

Chapter Six

Nadir

White lines disappeared beneath my bike as I headed away from the clubhouse with little regard for lanes. Wind flattened my jacket to my chest while Summer clung to my back beneath the rising sun. A warm spot grew where she contacted my body, leaving me craving for more of her. I pressed a reassuring hand over hers where she clasped my stomach in a death grip.

Businesses turned into residences. We zoomed past houses until I turned onto a familiar street I'd played on as a kid, dodging sparse traffic on a homemade billy cart before I was old enough to acquire my own bike.

Daffodils bloomed in merry rows before a fence that needed painting. I noted the job, mentally making time in my week to come back and run through a list of what Mama needed done. If Summer was staying here, then I'd have plenty of reasons to return. I'd thrown her into the deep end without warning and less choice, though to be fair, I'd claimed her to keep her safe.

Liar, liar.

Fine. I'd claimed her to keep anyone else's hands off her because I wanted her. Something soul-deep in me called to her, and I'd never experienced a pull like that before. Zenith's unspoken reminder to give her fair warning of what it meant to be an Old Lady rang in my head. Shaking it off, I pulled up at the curb, not wanting to damage Mama's lawn.

She was overprotective of three things: her foster children, fresh cookies, and her grass. Touching any of those things with an intent to steal or do damage and the wrath of a sixty-two-year-old woman would rain hell and brimstone on your day.

I stopped the bike and hung my helmet over the handlebars. Summer sat frozen behind me, stiff as a statue. Her fingers tightened on my ribs as I killed the engine. I grazed my knuckles over them; she was ice cold. Swearing softly, I picked her fingers loose one at a time, twisting to gather her in my arms. She shivered waves of tremors that washed over her too-thin frame as I tugged her helmet over her head and stowed it in the top box at the rear of my bike.

Her teeth chattered away, and her skin was cool beneath my palms.

"I'm so sorry, babe." I kissed each cheek, then her nose.

She blinked, raising her still-vague gaze to meet mine, though her eyes cleared to an island

60

blue as she focused on me. A small giggle escaped her, and she bit her lip.

I kissed it, tugging the soft skin free with my tongue, and kissed her deeply. Her giggle transformed into a soft sigh, and it was a balm to my blackened soul. "Never apologize for laughing, Summer. You're all the more beautiful for it."

"Thank you," she whispered and leaned into my touch.

Her head tilted back, her body softening in my arms. I kissed her again, sweeping my lips over hers in soft brushes that she returned. Blood surged to my cock. Pushing my arousal back, I cradled her in my arms, reveling in the gentle pressure of her body pressed flush to mine.

"You never have to be afraid again, Summer. You're mine, as long as you want to be." The words made my throat ache almost as much as my cock. I refused to keep a woman who didn't want to be with me, but I sure as hell wanted her to give us a chance.

She nodded, her gaze thoughtful. Dirty blonde strands tumbled over her face, obscuring my view.

A screen door banged behind me. I slid off the bike, bringing her with me, and turned to face Mama.

"Kade. I'm glad you're home." Mama held out open arms.

I leaned into her embrace without letting go of Summer's hand and brushed a kiss over Mama's cheek. "I'll be back sometime this week to paint your fence," I promised. "Make a list of anything else you'd like me to do."

"You just got here." Mama swatted my shoulder. Her gaze fixed on a point just beyond it. "And who is this? Kade Ryan. You didn't tell your mama you had a girl." She tutted in a reproving manner, but her sweeping gaze missed nothing, and I knew she saw more than she said.

"This is Summer. Summer, this is Maria. The woman who raised me. Who named me."

Summer raised an eyebrow in silent question and leaned toward me. "For a man with no name you seem to have an awful lot of them."

Mama laughed and tucked Summer under her arm in her traditional fashion, resembling nothing more than a mother hen and nothing less than love personified. "You are welcome here. Kade will show you around—"

Her head turned, listening for something only a mother could hear, but she wasn't the only one. Summer's head raised, and she focused on the house. Her lips moved, but nothing came out.

Mama bustled off and disappeared through the door of the house without another word.

"Babe, I have to go back for church. Zenith wants to rip me a new one, and I should probably let him." I gave her a rueful grin.

She half-returned the gesture, though her gaze was fixed on the house. "Is this where I stay now?"

"Probably better than the clubhouse. I don't have much of a room there to offer you."

"Is that your only home?"

"I wouldn't call the clubhouse home, exactly. More like sleeping at an office or a barracks." I hesitated, wrapping an arm around her soft form, and brushed my hand lightly over her back, over the scars her stretchy top hid. "This is my home. I haven't needed anything else more than a room and a place to park my bike since I was a kid."

"You're a nomad who can't stop, and I had my home ripped from me and have to adjust to a nothingness life." She spoke the words to her feet.

I followed her gaze to her leather-encased legs, tracing the slim line of her calf with my gaze, wishing it was my tongue worshiping her instead.

She needs time.

And I'd give that to her. Still, I could leave her with a parting thought, one that might leave her burning in the same way I suffered, wanting her.

I tucked her hair back from her face and dipped my head to brush my lips over the shell of her ear. "If you want a place to stay beyond this, I'll make one for us, Summer. And keep the boots. They look good on you. I'll get the owner another pair. Or buy you a new pair, if that's what you want."

She looked up at me. The vagueness crept into her gaze again, a look I was beginning to associate with her being overwhelmed, which was all too easy to understand.

I cursed myself for pushing too far, too fast.

"I feel like a kept woman."

Breath whooshed between my teeth in a violent exhale.

Smooth, Nadir. Real smooth.

"Take the time you need, Summer. I'll come back for you in a few days. I've got some...things to settle." *Like finding the bastards who hurt you and ripping them limb from fucking limb before I start on their organs.*

Torture wasn't my game; we had an enforcer for that. But there were some things a man had to handle for himself.

Summer held my gaze, searching. Whatever reflected there sent her spiraling back into her internal retreat. I pulled her into my chest, crushing her to me, and pressed my lips to her hair.

For a moment she stood stock-still, and I thought I'd lost whatever tenuous connection had grown between us, our strange brand of intimacy. A sigh slipped from her, and her arms rose in a tentative touch, sliding beneath my cut. Her cheek rested against my heart as her body shook yet again. I didn't have to see her face to know she was crying.

"Does she understand? You promised that girl things that are outside her frame of reference."

"I did." I considered. "But there was no way in hell I was letting you between her legs and then toss her aside when you were done."

"I don't toss women aside." Zenith's eyes narrowed. "But once I saw her back, we would have been hellbent on this path in any case, brother."

"Well, now she's got me instead of you." I paused. The thought hit me full on. I turned it over, weighed it up, and deemed the risk worthy. "*Would* you have claimed her, knowing what she'd been through?"

Pres held my unflinching gaze for a long moment then let out a barking laugh the brothers would have heard at the other end of the bar. "Fuck, no. You can keep your crazy outta my office. No more damn marriage counseling. You gonna ask her?"

I jerked my head. "Maybe. If she chooses it."

"You'd let her go if that's what she wants?"

It was a loaded question on both sides. Zenith faced off with me across his desk. However I answered this, he'd hold me to it. I pushed away from the doorframe, straightening to my full height.

"Whatever she chooses, brother. But I'll damn well keep trying to convince her to stay." I scratched my jaw and dropped the bomb I'd been turning over for the past few hours. "Might start looking for a place of my own. I've got cash stashed away from years of working for your ass. Never had a place to spend it before."

I held my breath and waited for Zenith's mouth to hit the deck. But in true fashion, he swung that one around to bite me in the ass.

"'Bout fucking time you settled down. What? You don't think I put thirteen-something years into grooming you as my succession plan to let you waste away in a club room? Fuck me, boy. I taught you better than that." Zenith leaned back in his chair and laced his hands behind his head.

I shook my head and turned for the door. A small smile I couldn't deny crept across my face. "Who's counting?"

Zenith's laughter followed me through the bar.

Chapter Seven

Summer

I curled into a ball on a slightly saggy bean bag reading a story about a sheep and a dog. Chester propped against my lap, chugging his bottle that sat in a squeezy sort of cage his tiny hands could grasp. I tilted it up a tiny amount to give him volume, and he rewarded me with a loud, milky burp.

Blue eyes that already held knowledge of the world they shouldn't have at his age surveyed me, albeit from an upside-down perspective.

"You're going to make me dizzy, little man." I smiled as he blinked, though my heart ached for him. "Yes, I miss her too. Did you know that your mother had the most beautiful voice? She used to sing you to sleep before they—" A sob built in my throat, and I slammed my lips shut before it could break free.

Chester jerked in my arms. His bottom lip wobbled, and I took the opportunity to slide the nib of his bottle between them.

"Comfort eating is just fine for your age group," I told him, swiping at the tears that rolled over my cheeks with my knuckles.

Would there be a day when I didn't cry? I'd gone from a soon-to-be-married, enthusiastic, though somewhat nerdy, college student to recovering from mental and physical abuse, caring for a dead woman's baby, and an outlaw biker's girlfriend.

That last was in serious question as I hadn't spoken to Kade—*Nadir*—whoever he wanted to be called in a few weeks.

He had been to the house to speak to Maria early several mornings but was gone by the time I emerged from the shower, clean and fresh, with only the distant purr of his bike and a freshly painted fence as evidence he had been here at all.

That, and his gifts.

Clothes for Chester and me. Shoes. The occasional squishy toy. Creams I assumed were for my back. Every one broke my already shattered heart. His compassion and absence broke me more than any whip had done before, but I refused to crumble.

Survive.

It was my word. I focused on it every day. Maybe one day that word would change, but I couldn't quite accept a steady state of being. Not yet. I kept expecting my world to be ripped apart yet again, though maybe it already was.

Zenith had wanted me to tell him who hurt us, the stolen women. But no matter how many times I tried in the mirror, I couldn't make myself form the names. So I drew them. Each sneer, every flicker of greed, hate and ruin. Their faces filled the paper Maria left me for the first week until I ran out of faces to draw. Then, one day, they were gone.

And Nadir still hadn't spoken to me.

Family betrays.

He had left me—left *us*—the moment I had held Chester. Nadir was an orphan from a family who had fallen off the face of the earth from what I had learned from Maria's unorthodox household. Kade Ryan was something of a legendary figure to the kids who free-ranged throughout the cottage and the yard. Each adored him, and from all accounts, he adored them right back, taking them for rides and pushing for charities that benefited each of them in some small way.

The concept of an uncle figure sat at odds to the man I knew, the *little* of him that I recognized. He'd claimed me in front of his boss, which had a meaning I still wasn't certain about. He had given me a place to stay that included a bed of my own and a hot shower—and oh, what a shower—as promised. But the man himself had been absent from the moment I had arrived in my new home, as though handing me over was enough.

Responsibility done, and hands washed clean.

Maria draped a dark blue cable knit blanket over us and extracted the bottle from Chester's hands. I tried not to startle as I gazed down at his sleeping form and settled back beneath his small, welcome weight. The book dropped from my hand, and Maria collected that too.

"Thank you," I whispered over Chester's sleeping form. "You have given us so much."

"You've lost enough, child." Maria's compassion-filled smile brought on a fresh wave of tears.

I blinked them back. "I can never repay this."

"I don't collect children to be repaid, Summer." Maria planted herself on the floor at my side. Colored shawls and tassels flowed around her in an ocean of color. "I give them a place to start their life. That is all. Kade is ready to leave, now," she mused.

"Nadi—Kade," I corrected myself. *Too many names.* "He hasn't been back to see me since—"

"He is giving you time. And I think he needs his time, too. That boy fights for everyone except for himself. Always first to help and last to leave."

"Does he ever sleep?" I smiled at the thought of the long-haired big, bad biker as a boy.

74

"Not as much as he should." Maria's tone turned tart, and I hid a smile. "He feels he has no place in the world because he doesn't know where he came from. And he said you were good with languages," she added.

I raised an eyebrow. "I studied. At university. Sort of." The thought of never completing my degree should have hurt, but that life seemed worlds away from who I was fast becoming. Chester took my time, and I loved watching and helping the younger children thrive.

The older ones I helped with schoolwork. Those who went to school. Some seemed to not have a social history, and I still wasn't sure how that worked. But every part of me trusted that Nadir and Maria fought for the children's safety and wellbeing over everything else.

This home was a haven, and though it was nothing like my own upbringing, I knew we were safer here than anywhere else in the world.

"It has been a big help to the children to have you here. And your time to teach them what you know."

"A lot is academia. I'm not sure how *useful* that information is." My new world had shown me what was practical in a school sense and what wasn't. Though I still nerded out with the bigger kids over obscure facts, the basics of reading and writing were more critical to the kids around me. My old life was frivolous in the face of the care Maria gave to her extended family when mine couldn't even bother to keep me.

That part was numb, and no matter how I tried to feel anything for it, I couldn't. It was just...gone. A kettle of tainted worms I'd have to face one day, perhaps, but not now. Maybe, if I managed to reconnect with Nadir, not alone.

"You miss him. He misses you." Maria pushed herself up from the floor with a soft groan. "These old bones. If you would like to put your research talents to use, there are boxes of files in the spare room at the end of the hall that need to be sorted. Boxes and boxes. One might even have Kade's name on it." She meandered from the room bearing a slight limp before I could formulate an answer for her.

Chester burbled in his sleep. I resettled both of us, knowing there was no way I could push myself up from the depths of the bean bag without waking him. Lying about doing little had never been part of my make-up, but the thought of closing my eyes in a safe environment for a moment held significant appeal.

Promising myself I'd check out the boxes Maria had mentioned later, I rested my head back and let the bean bag take my emotional weight, if only for a moment.

I slept longer than I intended and by the time I woke, the house was full, and Chester was nowhere to be seen. My arms were empty without his small weight, though my shoulders appreciated the break.

The scent of cookies brought me to the kitchen where Maria raged a battle against toddlers reaching for fresh game. Her spatula swatted grabbing hands in gentle taps though she wielded her weapon like a maestro.

"Ah, you're up. Here—" Maria thrust a pair of oven mitts in my direction, followed by a steaming tray of cookies.

"Where's Chester?" I donned the gloves with haste.

Maria pointed over her head to where Chester slept in a cradle he was fast growing out of at the back of the kitchen, barricaded by chairs and a small table.

We fell into the afternoon bake-and-make routine of after school hours that flowed seamlessly into dinner, and a shower turn around until the last child in complained of cold water.

"That's why I have a shower at five a.m.," I whispered.

A nose emerged from a hooded towel, followed by a raspberry blown in my direction. I patted the towel on the head and herded kids to their rooms. Rounds of evening stories began and though most shared a room or bunk so I could double up, by the time I met Maria at the end of the hall to a choir of snores it was well after my own bedtime.

Still, my gaze drew to the cluttered room at the end of the hall I'd assumed was full of randomly stored items.

Maria followed my look. "These old feet are going up, and the head is going down. Make sure you get sleep, Summer."

"Good night. And thank you. For everything." I squeezed her shoulders in a hug.

Maria bounced around with an energy that belied her age. "They will be up early, like you. Get rest," she admonished me. Her habitual smile graced her face, highlighting deep laugh lines that framed her mouth.

I only hoped I aged as beautifully.

"I will." It was a lie, and we both knew it, but she let me off the hook.

I checked in on Chester who slept in the corner of my room. Maria had moved an old cot, marred with the bite marks of many teething children, in and he slumbered away snug in his sleep sack. I brushed my fingers over his brow.

Would his biological family search for him? From what little I'd garnered from Amanda, he was as abandoned as the rest of us. She hadn't been sold, she had willingly gone with a mafia man, similar to the one I was originally sold to by all accounts. But her very white, middle-class family had disowned her for the action. The father had abandoned her to the fate I shared with all the girls.

A few had come to help out with the kids, but most preferred to stay at the club and dance there. I didn't shame them for their choices. They earned money there and were relatively safe, from what I was told. One of the girls offered to let me share her spotlight, but I'd declined saying I had two left feet when in all honestly, I didn't want to leave my safe little bubble of adopted family.

Of acceptance.

It couldn't last, my peace, and the thought of having to hand Chester over to a family who hadn't wanted him in the first place brought bile to my lips. I swallowed it back and pressed a kiss to his head.

The spare room held a bare mattress piled high with boxes. Dust motes filled the air when I flicked on the small overhead light. I perched on the corner of the mattress, tracking over the labels on each box.

One even has his name on it.

Maria had been intentionally vague about Nadir's past, and his need to both ignore and discover it. The dichotomy didn't escape me. Unable to find anything labeled Kade Ryan—I knew

Maria wouldn't have used his club name—I started at the nearest box.

Each file held personal details for children both present in the house and long gone. Over forty years of history existed in the small room, and by the time I was just over halfway through, my gaze was drooping, and I held a greater degree of awe than before for Maria's tenacity.

I hid a yawn behind my hand, determined not to stop, but my energy was fading fast. Gripping the edge of a box with a generic-looking name hand scrawled across the front, I opened the first file.

A faded Polaroid photograph of a long-haired boy with golden locks fell into my lap. I raised it to the light for closer inspection, but my heart knew I had found him. Adrenaline zinged through my veins. Energized, I flicked through the files that filled the box, devouring every fact and detail.

Paired with access on an archaic phone one of the older children Maria fostered had given me when he upgraded his own, I backed up the scant information the box provided with news articles and dates. On a whim, I checked if my university password still worked. The ancient languages facility shared the genealogy server. Where I'd once dived through names and origins for historical research, Nadir's jigsaw past formed into a tangible history laid out before me.

By the time I was finished, I knew more about who he had been than I knew about myself. I wondered at his avoidance of discovering his own history. Nadir had taken his nameless persona to a deeper degree and seemed to identify it.

Some part of me recoiled at the thought I was digging into something he might consider an invasion of his highly coveted privacy. Maria had sent me off on my path, and I trusted her to understand his needs better than my own scant impression of the man I was fast falling for, though I pushed that thought aside in an avoidance of my own making.

I flicked the light off, leaving the box tucked just inside the door so I could find it in the morning. Bypassing my bedroom, I headed for the kitchen. Maria and I had taken to sharing a pot of tea before bed, and though the house remained dark, I couldn't bring myself to break the ritual.

Slivers of starlight lit the room in a blue-gray haze. Feeling my way around the kitchen with my hands and half-closed eyes, I reached for the teapot and encountered hard bare flesh. My eyes snapped open in my second adrenaline rush of the evening, and my mouth dropped open ready to emit a scream that would shatter the quiet hours of the night.

A broad palm clapped over my mouth, stifling my cry. I slapped both hands forward and encountered a very bare chest. Denim grazed my legs as he herded me back against the bench, and lips brushed my ear. Leather and spice filled my senses in a familiar rush that flooded my body with desire and need, leaving me lightheaded. I stopped pushing against that chest and let my hands wander a little.

"I've missed you, Summer." Nadir pulled his hand from my mouth, and I breathed him in. "Shouldn't a good girl like you be in bed?" His knuckles grazed my cheek and traveled along the line of my throat to cup the back of my head as he drew me close.

A hot flush rushed over me and settled heavy between my legs. Need ached through me at his touch, at his whispered words that promise so much more than what he said. A shiver slid down my spine as I reacted to his touch.

My head swirled with the mixed scent of him and combined with the excitement of what I'd learned about him, I completely missed the obvious social cues right in front of me. My head tilted back, lips parted, I mentally sorted what information to give him first.

Nadir's fingers tightened in my hair, and his mouth crashed down over mine, stealing my breath and scattering every thought.

If I'd thought his first kiss had been soul-rending, this one was of the tear-off-my-panties-and-leave-me-drenched variety.

His body molded to mine as he clasped me to him. Nadir's mouth teased mine, alternating light grazes and harder, rougher caresses that left me gasping. He tugged on my hair, angling my head back the way he wanted. A soft cry broke from my lips, and he slid his tongue into my mouth, swallowing my moans.

Denim scraped my thighs. His knee pressed between them, and he tapped my feet apart, pressing against every sensitive nerve ending.

I gripped his shoulders and tore my mouth from his. "Nadir—"

"Shh, Summer. I need to feel you against me." He pressed my cheek to his bare chest, enveloping me in hard, corded muscle.

A shuddering breath left me as I leaned against him. "I missed you too."

"Did you." His voice was flat, void of emotion, and it took me a second to recognize he'd made it a statement, not a question. He retreated as fast as he'd come onto me, and the turnaround left me in a dizzying whirl.

"Yes?" I second-guessed myself in an instant. "I mean, I did. When you were here, by the time I cleaned myself up enough to be presentable, you were gone. You never came to see me." My breath hitched, caught in a maelstrom of emotion I'd held at bay for weeks. "Why didn't you come to see me?" *What did I do that was so wrong?*

"You got cleaned up for me?" His voice held a note of amusement.

Relief gusted over me that he'd reacted to something I'd said. Anything, no matter how. I couldn't handle the emotionless void he'd offered a moment before. "Yes. I had to."

"No, you don't," he corrected me.

"I do, actually. Ever since—" I pressed my lips together. *You can do this.* "Ever since you found me, I need to be clean and showered. Every day. It stops me feeling so..." I ran out of words and shrugged into his chest.

He swore softly, pressing a hard kiss to the top of my head. "Then shower all you like. And— I need to ask you something." He seemed to stop breathing. I held my breath too and had no idea why I was doing it. "The boy." He formed the words carefully. "Was he from your ex?"

I blinked at his bare chest. "What?"

"Chester," he snapped, his voice brittle with impatience and another emotion I couldn't identify. "Is he from your relationship with your ex? The one you were engaged to?"

"He's not mine," I said stupidly.

"Summer—"

"Chester. He's Amanda's baby. I— I took him on after they killed her. Are you going to take him away from me?" My vision blurred.

Not now, not again.

Life without Chester in it just wasn't possible.

84

"He's Amanda's baby," Nadir repeated my words. His hands flexed on my back. "How—" He swore again.

"Stop that," I whispered. "I told you about him. I'm sure I told you?" I was starting to doubt my own sanity.

"You might have missed a bit." Nadir held me tight to him.

"If you were around more, then maybe we'd be able to have a proper conversation," I snapped, then closed my eyes. "I'm so sorry. I'm never rude. I don't like conflict at all. I can't cope with it."

"Shhh. Oh, babe. No wonder you've been falling apart. I thought I was giving you time to heal, and I've screwed that all to hell."

"It's okay," I murmured into his chest. Heat radiated from him. I pressed a tentative kiss to his skin, and without thinking, licked at a spot there. He tasted of salt and diesel. The same scent he had when I first met him.

He let out a low groan that might have been a moan and tangled his fingers in my hair, massaging my scalp in sweeping circles. "No. Oh, hell no. It's so far from okay it's not fucking funny. It's me who's sorry, babe."

I swallowed hard and raised trembling fingers to brush over the hard lines of his face thrown into harsh relief by the slanted shards of light that filtered through the kitchen window. My fingertips came away damp. I frowned, pressing them together.

Dark liquid covered them. I stifled a gasp and turned him to the bluish light that penetrated the kitchen in shards. Blood—I assumed it was blood—covered half his face. I felt around behind me for a cloth and dabbed it to his cheek.

Nadir stood passive as I ministered to him.

"What happened to you? Where's the cut?" I dabbed frantically.

There was so much of the stuff smeared across his face and into his stubble, but I couldn't find the wound. I checked over his eyebrow, rising onto my tiptoes to peer at him in the dim light. Wasn't that where boxers got hit and bled a lot? I swiveled around, searching for the light switch.

Nadir caught my wrist when I reached out.

"It's not mine."

"I need to clean you up and see if there's any infection." Infection I knew about. We were on intimate terms, and I didn't want him to go through that.

"Summer." He turned me back to him, his hands closed in fists around mine, imprisoning me. "It's not mine."

His words finally sank in.

My mouth dried. "Then who?"

He squeezed my hands. "I'm going to have a shower. Then I want to take you somewhere."

"Where?"

The corner of his mouth moved, but in it was the side darkened by shadow and I couldn't see if he was smiling or not. "It's a surprise."

Nadir left me standing in the kitchen, and a few moments later I heard the shower running, though no light had turned on. He was back with me faster than I expected while I tried to comprehend the transition from his searing kiss to his abrupt departure. Who the fuck came home covered in blood?

My boyfriend. Apparently.

I shook my head at my new world, a bug who had skimmed out beyond the waves and couldn't make her way back to shore.

He stood before me dressed in a clean white tee and fresh jeans. No blood in sight, thankfully. "Do you have a jacket? Shoes?"

"You know I do." I held his gaze for a defiant second.

His lips pursed. "Then get them." He caught my hand, squeezing gently.

Swallowing my misgivings, I darted into my room, checked Chester, and left a scrawled note for Maria, though I knew she'd likely wake when Nadir's bike started. I returned to his side in silence.

Nadir's hand closed around my waist. He gave me a hard jerk, pulling me into his side. Fingers dug into my skin. He kissed me like he was a starving man, and I was the last food left for him. My head spun as he released me and strode toward the door.

A questioning glance over his shoulder left me to follow in his wake, shaking my head about why I wasn't putting up a fight, though it was well after midnight. I'd spent hours helping to get the household to sleep and I refused to wake them all on a whim.

I slipped my jacket on as he closed the door behind me, locking out the residual warmth the cottage offered. The night air held a decent chill and the day dress I'd never changed out of wasn't up to the task. I clutched my jacket to me as he mounted his bike and held out a helmet.

"Nadir—"

"Please, Summer." His voice—was that a plea?

The thought of him begging for anything struck me as funny. Nadir was far more a take-what-I-want man from what I had seen.

I pushed the helmet over my head and choked on hair. "There has to be a better way to do this."

Huffing his own laugh, Nadir helped free me from my homemade noose. He sorted me out, tidied up my hair, and placed the helmet back on my head. Both of us were in fits of stifled giggles by the time I was ready.

"You are certainly something else, babe," Nadir said dryly. He held out a hand.

I stared at it for a second as the ground swayed beneath me. Going with him, away from the house, suddenly seemed like a really bad idea. But he had never given me a reason not to trust him, had provided for both Chester and me with gifts...I shook my head inside the helmet.

Every time Nadir swept into my life, he changed things in ways I was prepared to accept. Everything moved so fast with him. But I'd come this far, and his expectant gaze weighed on me.

Swallowing hard, I placed my hand in his and climbed onto the back of his bike.

The same as he had on my first—and only—ride on a motorcycle, Nadir wrapped my hands around his waist and gave them a gentle squeeze.

"Hold tight," he murmured over the familiar purr of the engine.

Then we were gone.

Chapter Eight

Nadir

*H*aving Summer on the back of my bike again felt damn good. Her grip wasn't quite at strangulation level this time, but her warmth pressed to my back gave me hope. Once suburbia and the outskirts of the township fell away behind us, I gunned the engine, looking for the turn I'd mapped out a hundred times in my head in the last few weeks, though I'd only visited the place once.

The corner came up faster than I remembered. I took it, slowing over the potholes that littered the unsealed surface. The dirt road forked. I headed along the left arm, through thickly treed forest that blotted out residual starlight.

The road ended in a flattened area. I killed the engine, and turned to help Summer out of her helmet, but she already had it off. I supposed the fiasco of earlier hadn't helped.

"Where are we?" Summer stared around the clearing, the helmet clutched to her stomach.

I extracted the hardware from her hands and stowed it away, exchanging it for a picnic blanket and a softer, warmer mink blanket. Bundling them under one arm, I slid my other around her waist and lifted her to the ground. "I found this place by accident but sort of fell in love with it. There's a river here—" I gripped her hand a little too tight and drew her to the far side of the clearing where water bubbled along, heedless of the dark night. "And when the sun rises there," I pointed to the east, "it casts this whole area aglow in pink and peach."

"Peach? I'm not sure I took you as a romantic." Her voice was muted, but it held the edge of teasing.

I clung to that poor strand of thought to keep myself afloat. Finding a flat patch of ground, I knelt and laid out the rugs. "I know I haven't been around much for the past few weeks, but I've been trying to get my head together. I thought you might appreciate time. To...think. I don't know." I shoved my hair back with one hand, staring up at her from where I knelt on the picnic blanket. Moonlight cast her face in shadow. I held out a hand. "Sit with me?"

Summer knelt beside me. Her feet curled under her as she sank to the rug, her arms wrapped around herself. "It's beautiful," she murmured. "But why are we here in the middle of the night?"

"I—" I paused. Taking her away from her bed at this time suddenly seemed selfish and thoughtless. "I wanted you to myself, and not to have to share what time we have together. I can take you back?" I offered, though my heart clenched.

"I like it here." Her fingers brushed the back of my hand.

My heart leaped. "Good." I cleared my throat. "It's yours. Ours."

"I found something—"

Our words collided, and it took me a moment to separate them. "You first."

"No, you go. What did you mean, it's ours?"

I took a deep breath and wound my arms around her, needing her soft form against me. "I couldn't stop thinking about you. Every day, while I was working for the club. Every night when I was in my room, and you weren't there. So I went for a ride. This place had a for sale sign up. I bought it. The land. I thought— I remembered you said you wanted to have somewhere to stay." I stumbled over the words in my haste, each thought tumbling in front of the next in a muddle. "I know there's nothing here, and I remembered you said you wanted more than to stay with Maria, to do something to help the girls like you. The rescued ones. So. We can build a house, a dorm, or a restaurant. Whatever it is you want to do. It's yours. I just want to share it with you." My heart hammered in my chest, and by the time I was finished, I was out of breath.

Summer surveyed me quietly. "That's quite a speech."

The corners of my lips rose. "Probably the longest I've ever made," I agreed.

"But...I didn't say any of that to you. I said it to Maria. Weeks ago."

My mouth dried. "I know."

"Mmm."

Was that a good sound or a bad one? I had no idea. My hands flexed on her back. "I know it's bare right now, but I can do whatever you need. I've got skills, and I've got money. I've never used what I've earned except to help Mama out." I babbled on, worse than a school kid in front of a headmistress about to receive his first caning, and not the enjoyable sort.

"Nadir."

"If you want to live here with the girls, upskill them, whatever, I don't have to be here. You said you—"

"Kade."

It was the first time she had used the name Maria had given me, and that alone halted my overabundance of babble. Apparently once I started speaking, it was hard to shut the floodgates. I hoped it wouldn't be a permanent condition, or Zenith might get punch happy.

"Yeah?"

"I love it. And I'd love to build something with you."

"You would?"

"Yes." She scooted a little closer, climbing onto my lap with a tentative touch as though asking permission with each movement. "And I don't want to do it alone."

Air whooshed from my lungs. I scooped her onto my lap. Her knees slid over my hips until she straddled me, and I held her pressed tight to me. "I'm not good at this relationship thing. I've never had one before. And I have no idea what the fuck I'm doing," I confessed.

"And I only have damaging relationships with people who discard me." She rolled her eyes. "So, you know, we're a great match."

"Oh, we'll have loads of fun." I squeezed her waist.

Summer laughed. Her head tilted back, and starlight lit the column of her throat to where the sliver of skin disappeared beneath the scalloped neckline of her dress.

I hardened beneath her. Heat from her seared me through my jeans. My hands dropped to her hips, gathering the material there into bunches that exposed a smooth expanse of thigh. My heart rate sped up for a different reason.

Her hands brushed my shoulders. She leaned forward, letting me take her weight as she shifted against me. Her hips rocked forward and back, and it took me a moment to recognize her rhythm.

"Babe." I stilled her motion in a firm grip at her hips, fighting a mental battle between what I craved and what she needed. "Are you sure—"

"Yes. I'm sure." She pressed her lips to mine in an open-mouthed kiss that drove all conscious thought from my mind.

The tip of her tongue traced my lips, and I took that as a personal invitation. I dropped her dress and ran my hands from her thighs to her neck, tangling my hands in her hair. My tongue danced with hers in a slow rhythm designed to drive up both mad with need.

Her soft mewls against my mouth amped my arousal to the point of painful. Her hips rocked over me, the thin barrier of her panties grazing over the hard ridge of my jeans where my aching cock strained for release.

I slid the jacket from her shoulders, baring her body encased in a thin, cotton sundress to me. She lifted her hands over her head. The movement raised her breasts to the perfect height. I caught her arms between my hands, pinning them up. My lips teased her nipples through the cotton, alternating hard flicks with my tongue against not so gentle nips until she was a writhing hot-as-fuck mess on my lap, already coming half undone. I tugged the dress over her head and grazed my hands down her back, memorizing every ridge of scarred flesh there.

Summer froze. Her body became a taut line, her eyes wild when I drew back to look at her.

I cupped her cheeks, forcing her to meet my gaze. "You are fucking beautiful. Every single part of you." I kissed her mouth gently, sweetly, then moved over her body, kissing the tops of her breasts, twisting her on my lap to kiss the scars that crisscrossed her back.

"No—" Her nails dug into my shoulder, and she bit the muscle there on a half sob, hiding beneath her hair.

I traced the fainter lines that curled around her ribs and beneath her breasts with my mouth. "All of you is beautiful. Every part, Summer. And I love you."

"You can't love me. You don't know me." Her voice was muffled in my shoulder.

I grazed my chin against her cheek, urging her to look at me. When she lifted her head, I claimed her mouth in a kiss that left us both swaying where we sat. "I fucking love you, and I'd do anything for you." I let my eyes give her the promise I'd already fulfilled but couldn't voice just yet. "Hell, girl. I'll marry you if that's what you need. Anything."

Her half sob became full-blown as she launched forward, kissing me frantically.

A harsh laugh bubbled in my chest amidst failing limbs. I rolled us both, pinning her beneath me, and shucked my shirt over my head. It hit the dirt, somewhere. I didn't care where. The drive to have her bare flesh pressed to mine overwhelmed everything.

I kissed her hard, sliding my tongue into her mouth to match the rhythm I built, pressing my jean-covered hips into her thinly veiled pussy. Her ass filled my palms perfectly. I slid them over her lace panties, ones I'd bought for her, lifting her lithe form only to grind into her soft flesh.

Her head dropped back onto the blanket. Soft pants left her lips, her sighs driving me higher. I slid my fingers between us, pushing past the thin barrier of her panties, and sank them slowly between her swollen, sensitive folds, teasing her entrance. Her sighs became moans as arousal slicked my fingers in cream, and I groaned aloud.

"Fuck, girl. You're soaked."

"Please, Kade." Her legs lifted, winding around my waist and hips, arching into my touch.

My breath stalled. "Say it again," I grated.

"Please, Kade, please—"

"Since you're so fucking pretty when you beg." I bared my teeth and thrust two fingers knuckle-deep into her slicked flesh, flicking my thumb over her clit.

She screamed, unraveling beneath me in a matter of seconds. Her hot little pussy clenched and fluttered around my fingers as I worked her over, driving her from one orgasm to the next. Her hips jerked, her cries painfully haunting.

I stripped off my jeans with one hand, leaving the other still inside her, and felt around the pockets for my wallet.

"You— you don't need one," she gasped. "I can't— he made sure I couldn't—"

I swore hard and loud above her, then claimed her mouth in a punishing kiss. "You will never hurt again, Summer. I promise you." I teased her tender, puffy pussy lips with gentle strokes, grazing her clit with my roughened knuckles. Her hips bucked against me, and when I was sure she was on edge again, I fisted myself and slid the head of my cock into her.

She stiffened with a low cry that sliced my heart.

You fucking idiot.

"Summer. Am I hurting you? Tell me." I caught her chin, making her look at me.

Her glazed eyes lanced straight through me. She brought her heels to my ass and pushed, hard. "I need you inside me. Deep. Please—"

I sank balls deep into her and buried my head in the crook of her neck with a low groan. "Fuck, Summer—"

She shifted, her hips jerking, and I already recognized the pulsing pattern of her pussy. I pushed harder into her then withdrew, setting a steady, fast pace designed to keep her orgasming. The double edge was that it pushed me toward my own pleasure that I refused to acknowledge, though she clamped around me again and again. Tendrils clung to her sweat-soaked skin as she crossed her ankles behind my back, lifting her hips to take me deeper.

My thrusts changed, urgency riling me. I roared her name as I came, arched over her. She shivered, fluttering around me in a series of tiny aftershocks, and our cries mingled, breaking the silence of the night.

I wrapped the heavy extra blanket around us both and curved my body around hers to provide extra warmth. Summer sighed, nestling into my arms. The invisible walls I'd erected between us for a stupid reason crumbled as I held her close to me.

"I can't wait to sleep with you every night." I trailed kisses from the corner of her mouth, over her cheek, and nibbled at the soft spot beneath ether ear, smiling when she squeaked. "Every. Night."

"With emphasis on sleep?" She cracked one dozy eye open, her lips turned up in a sexy-as-sin smile.

"Maybe." I kissed her deeply, aching with every soft sound she made.

Mine. She's mine.

"Good." She sank into my chest, and the next soft sound she made was a purr that healed the cracks in my heart.

I let her sleep, watching the darkness fade with the false dawn. As sunlight crested the horizon, Summer stirred. I looked down to find her watching me.

"You're right. It is beautiful," she murmured, holding my gaze with her ocean blue one.

"You're looking in the wrong place," I pointed out.

She shook her head. "I'm not." She lifted her head for a kiss I provided with enthusiasm. Her fingers rose to her lips, swollen from our night of lovemaking. "I have something to tell you." She looked right through me with those eyes.

I fell and kept on falling.

"Me too." I kissed her again. "Last night, before I came to you—"

"I know your name."

"What?"

"I know who you are, Nadir."

Chapter Nine

Nadir

*S*he knows my name.

My world stalled and I shook my head again, barely able to focus on her whisper.

"I know where you came from." Desperation drove her voice to a higher pitch. "Please—" She reached up, grazing soft fingers over my cheek.

I wanted to nuzzle into them, but I lay there, frozen into stone. "I don't think it's the right time for begging, babe." My heart thundered in my chest, so loud I had no idea what I was saying.

Summer took a deep breath. "Your name. It's Jason Brian Peterson."

"You know my name?" Wonder filled my voice.

I stared at her, her wild curls tumbling around her face in a hot mess, her soft pink lips parted. But it was her aqua blue eyes that held me captive, unable to move.

She knows my fucking name.

After not knowing for so long, the thought of having that information was both precious and abhorrent to me. Whatever it was, I could live without it.

I rolled away from her, staring blindly into a piece of wilderness I'd bought to secure a home for two lost people only to find that apparently I didn't need it.

The ground wavered beneath me, and this time my freefall had nothing to do with her.

Okay, it had a *lot* to do with her, but not for the same reasons as before.

Don't you want to know who you are?

No more made-up names, no more names I had given myself, or earned, trying over the years to make something that was never meant to be mine fit.

Morning sounds of birds rising with the sun filtered back to me, grounding me. *No.* I knew who I was, and who I was meant to be. Knowing my history wouldn't change that.

So why couldn't I face this head-on, as I did everything else in my life?

"I don't need to know." I spoke to the edge of the tree line, still facing away from her. Hiding.

"Scared, are you?" Her voice was rueful, but it might as well be a smack in the face from a club girl on a cold night.

I rolled back to face her and let my fury, pent-up for so damn long, have full reign. "*Scared?* I pull you out of the hell you were in, you and Chester—" The orphan's name got stuck in my chest, somewhere around where my heart was meant to be, but I pushed through it. "I pull you out of that, face off with the men who hurt you, Summer, who flayed your back. Do you want to know what I did to them? Every. Single. One who hurt you?"

"No—" she stuttered a half sound, but I spoke over her.

"I did exactly what I promised you. Those men paid for their sins with each pound of flesh on their bodies. They screamed, and I enjoyed it. Do you know *why*, Summer? Because I thought about you the entire time. I thought of your screams, of what you didn't show them, what they tried to get out of you with each whip mark and I made sure as fuck they screamed louder and longer than any of them ever made you."

The color left her face at my words and the light in those stunning ocean blue-green eyes dimmed.

The perverse, righteous desire to lash out died in an instant, and I held out my arms.

She flinched.

Flinched.

I had done that.

"Fine. You're right. I'm a fucking coward, and I don't want to face it. Better off not knowing at all, right?" It was the mantra I'd clung to for so long that I wasn't sure I could pry myself free. I pushed my hair off my face, raking my nails through my scalp just to *feel*, unable to keep the snarl out of my voice.

Her breath hitched.

I closed my eyes, not wanting to watch her get dressed and walk away from me.

Stupid, stupid, fucking stupid—

"It's okay." Soft, gentle arms wrapped around me. Her bare body pressed to my chest, and she nuzzled there. No tremors, no tears. Unafraid. "Thank you. It's okay to be scared, and you're the last person I would ever say is a coward. Not after what you did for me and all those women. Girls, really, with their futures ripped away. And their pasts." She tilted her head back to survey me with those ocean-deep eyes. "But you don't have to lose yours, too."

My arms closed around her acceptance of all the fucked-up things and I was in gratitude she hadn't run for the hills. I grazed my fingers over her cheek, reveling in the sweet smile she gave me. Breath left me in a rush that I blew over her head in a harsh exhale. "You know, you're taking what I said awfully well."

"A few of my priorities were rearranged over the last six months. I've learned what I thought love and respect meant, only to find that they didn't. And I've discovered a different kind of love that sort of suits me." She peeked at me from beneath her lashes. "The rest I'm still coming to terms with. Maybe...I'd like some help with that."

I gave her a jerky nod. "I can do that." Hell, if she could balls up and face far worse things, then I wasn't about to let her fly solo. "Okay. Give me..." I pressed my lips together, unable to make myself push the words past them.

Chicken shit.

Summer nodded, a small smile playing at the corners of her lips. "You were born Jason Brian Petersen, April third, nineteen ninety-nine to Marcus and Nancy Petersen who apparently lived a very good life, were comfortable, and absolutely loved their infant son. He was a bank manager, and she ran a small cafe all on her own, with her husband's support. She had blonde hair, like yours. They lived in the next town over if you want to drive by their house. And I— I have pictures."

"You do, huh?" I stroked a trembling finger down her cheek.

"Yes." She caught my hand in hers and kissed it fiercely.

The thought of my parents together in a photo bloomed something warm and all-encompassing in my chest.

Jason Brian Petersen.

They lived just around the corner.

Lived.

I stopped practicing the name that fit me fine, as well as any other I'd acquired in my lifetime, and focused on her.

"What happened to them?" The wonder slipped, and my voice came out harsher, raw at the edges.

"Back then there was some small, organized crime in the city, a fledgling unit that was shut down fast, but not before the bank was robbed. Well, someone tried to rob it. And that day, Nancy was visiting her husband at work, bringing him the same sandwich that she made for him nearly every working day for over twenty years. They were both killed in the attempted robbery. I'm sorry, Kade, but I don't know who did it. I—I couldn't find that out." She stared up at me with huge doe eyes glistening with unshed tears.

For me.

Something lodged in my throat and for the second time in my few weeks with her, I found my heart.

"You're amazing." I brushed my fingertips over her brow, and miraculously they weren't shaking.

She nuzzled my hand a little. "I wanted to find out more."

"You've done plenty, babe." I tugged her light form tighter into my arms with little resistance, kissing the top of her head. *I have a name.* My arms tightened around her as I crushed her to my chest, squeezing far too tight. "You've given me everything, do you know that? Everything. And I damn well love you for it."

"I wanted to make you happy. You gave me back everything too, you know. I was so desperate when you found me, and I was so lost." Summer drew back from my embrace, her arms still wound around me. Tears blurred her eyes and tracked her cheeks in a deluge that erupted.

After everything that had happened to her, she finally let her guard down. I cupped the back of her head with one hand, drawing her chin back as I stared into her aqua blue eyes, stroking my thumb over her bottom lip.

Her pupils dilated as she drew in a long breath, her wide-eyed gaze fixed on me.

"Listen to me, Summer. You do make me happy. And I absolutely love you. Just having you in my life is a blessing."

"I think I come with extra baggage."

"You mean Chester?" I drew back to stare into her eyes. "Babe, do you think I'm asking you to give him up?"

"Are you?"

"Hell, no. The world doesn't need more orphans."

"I didn't have the best set of parents in the world as role models."

"Then we work it out together." I pressed her back on the rug, leaning forward to lick the tops of her breasts.

She shivered. Goosebumps broke out, pebbling her skin. Her nipples tightened, and I sucked one into my mouth, teasing and flicking while I rolled the other between my fingers.

"Jason—"

I lifted my head. "No. You call me by the names my family uses. Both of them. Either. I'm not some name on a birth certificate, Summer. I'm the man you see before you. Nothing more, nothing less."

She nodded and shifted beneath the blanket. "Nadir. Kade." She gave me a coy look through her lashes. "You'll have to make sure which name sounds best when I scream it." Her fingers curled around my cock, giving me light strokes that drew a long groan from my throat.

"Then I'd better start testing that out." I kissed her, sliding my hand over her stomach to thighs slicked with her arousal, and began to work out which of my names I wanted her to use.

Well today, anyway.

About the Author

USA Today Bestselling author Sofia Aves writes fast-paced police romances, sizzling military units, steamy cowboys with a Montana backdrop and the occasional cheeky god. She loves reading Indie authors and hides her collection of college romance books beneath an ever-growing TBR pile. Sofia is the marketing manager for Romance Writers of Australia and has a regular author marketing column in their monthly magazine. She writes kidlit for charity and has over eighty publications across three not-so-super-secret pen names.

Sofia is a mum of three crazies in a returned veteran household, and has an overly large fur baby who thinks she's a teacup puppy. After eighteen years of planning and dreaming, Sofia and her husband will put the finishing touches on their very own alpaca park this year. Sofia lives near Brisbane, Australia.

Sign up to Sofia's newsletter and get a free Blue Blooded Brothers book.

Haven't read the Z Boy's prequel? Get it for free here:

A TABLE FOR TEN

www.sofiaves.com

Follow Sofia on

OTHER SERIES BY SOFIA AVES

Blue Blooded Brothers

Red Hart Ranch

Texan Devils

Christmas Romance

Shortbread Shakedown

Secret Santa

Paranormal Romance

Trickster's Law

A Portrait in Ash & Lace

Acknowledgments

The Bleeding Souls Saved By Love authors *finally* got me to write a motorcycle club book! I've had a ball being in Nadir's head, and Summer was the perfect, sweet foil for his blackened heart.

While I was organizing the final touches and polishing my Wicked Warriors story, we had Covid running through our house, alongside a few other choice viruses. Kudos to my family for putting up with me thrashing out the words and for my Miss8 who batted out unicorn headdresses and occasionally snored while I typed frantically beside her.

Thank you to Lisa for taking a chance on an author you didn't know to give me beautiful editing and to Jess for making up Nadir's stunning cover. I greatly appreciate you both.

My crit chicks - as always, you girls are my backbone! Thank you for helping me step out of my light gray comfort zone and dive headlong into something darker. I don't think I'll be emerging any time soon.

Sofia xx

Peter's Prize Sneak Peak

Candi Fox

Belle checked her appearance in the mirror one last time. She looked the part of a young twenty something rich girl. The designer red dress hugged her curves. Rubies and diamonds sparkled at her wrists and ears. A half-inch red ribbon collar graced her neck. Made from the same material as her dress. The scarlet color stood out against her perfect pale skin. Five-inch red stiletto heels finished her outfit.

She grabbed the small red clutch and headed out the door to the waiting limo. A classic white Rolls Royce from the forties. Dante, the driver, opened the door before helping her in. He waited until she fastened her seat belt before closing the door and taking his own seat.

"Do you have everything you need, Miss Belle?"

Belle smiled. Dante was one of the people she liked. Even if he was on Peter's payroll, Dante had her back. If it came to a choice between the two, she honestly didn't know if Dante would choose her or Peter.

"I have everything I need. I'll meet you in the park at midnight."

"Call me if you need backup."

"If I need backup, Dante, I've failed."

He shook his head, expertly maneuvering the car into busy Baltimore traffic. After they were on the expressway, he rolled up the partition. Belle put in her wireless buds and hit play. The first strains of Chopin's 'Nocturnes' hit her ears. She used the ninety-minute drive to review the file on her target.

Paolo Segal, a soldier, was on his way to Capo for the Corsican mob. In his early forties, with dark hair, tanned skin and a full beard and mustache. Not a bad-looking man, but she knew he was a soulless scum sucking son of a bitch who dealt in underage girls.

Technically, she was taking out the piece of shit so Peter could garner favor from Alcide Roche, an underboss in a rival mob family. Roche would be in attendance tonight. Belle decided she would give him a personal trophy from Segal.

A shiver passed over her as they entered the city. How Peter lived in all this glass and steel she'd never know. Belle lived on Peter's estate an hour and a half outside the city. Acres of trees and foliage. Two years ago, Peter added gardens with a gazebo in the middle. A reward for a job well done.

Their relationship was complicated. She loved him and he owned her. A never-ending contract that should have ended after a hundred years.

The car came to a stop. She pulled out the earbuds, turning off her music. Dante opened the door, offering his hand to help her out. Paparazzi lined both sides of the red carpet rolled out for the ball. Tonight, the richest people in the city would all be under one roof. The elite rubbing elbows with prominent politicians and organized crime leadership.

D.C. was less than ninety minutes away. They would make tonight deals of epic proportions under the table. Elle smiled as she walked down the red camera. She took the proffered glass of champagne, blending in with the crowd.

Over the next hour, she mentally tagged not only her mark, but Alcide, Peter, and a few other notable faces. One of those was James Bruno, Peter's nemesis. James had his latest paramour on his arm. A twenty-something with dark hair. Belle didn't pay her a lot of attention. Bruno went through women like other people went through underwear.

She made her way through the crowd to Segal's area. Belle made sure she was in his periphery. A few minutes later, she joined in a conversation close to her mark. She smiled, laughed, and acted like she didn't have a care in the world. Totally spoiled rich girl without thought too much other than herself. Just his type.

It took him less than five minutes to make his way into the conversation. Someone introduced them. Belle offered her hand to Paolo.

"Pleasure to meet you, Mr. Segal."

"None of that," he replied. "Call me Paolo."

"Paolo it is. I'm Audra Dark. Please call me Audra."

"Dark, that name seems familiar. Is your father a banker or a businessman?"

"Both, actually."

"You must be Alastair Dark's youngest girl."

Belle smiled in reply. Keep it simple. Let them assume when it's beneficial. A little fae glamor and she looked the part. Belle's blonde hair was currently a deep chocolate brown. It hung loose down her back, brushing the curves of her ass. Her blue eyes were cocoa brown.

She watched Segal drink in her appearance, his eyes eating up the expensive outfit. He looked at the jewels she wore almost longer than he looked at her tits. Millions of dollars of rubies and diamonds graced her ears and wrists.

Belle watched as he grabbed two glasses of champagne, handing her one before taking a drink of his own. She batted her eyelashes and let a little giggle slip past her lips.

"Too much champagne and I'll simply lose my head. I should make this my last one. I've already had three."

Truth is, she had six, but her metabolism moved the alcohol through her system too fast for her to get drunk. They spent the next twenty minutes in idle chatter. Segal plied her with drink after drink, making sure she never had an empty glass in her hand. With each drink, she acted giddier. A little less sober.

His hand went to the small of her back. Segal leaned in. "Say, why don't we get some fresh air. That should help clear those champagne bubbles from your head."

She smiled and nodded her head, allowing him to lead her outside and into the gardens. He led her deep into the gardens, away from everyone else. Belle endured his light pawing and even one disgusting kiss. YUCK! I'm going to have to gargle with an entire bottle of bleach to get that taste from my mouth.

Ahh, bleach, a beautiful and wondrous invention with many uses.

Gargling not being one of them. Unless you want to inflict damage. She was all for that. Speaking of damage, it was time to take this ass clown down. Belle leaned into the kiss, giving it an Oscar worthy performance.

With a small use of magic, she called a wicked blade to her hand. While Segal grabbed her ass with both hands, kneading the flesh. Belle angled the blade with the flat edge toward his spine and used her preternatural strength to shove it deep into the base of his neck. A swift, hard pull back and she severed his spinal cord. A move she'd perfected over the years.

She caught his body twisting so he would land on the ground. As he breathed his last, she removed his signet ring from his finger. Belle left the dead body on the ground. Moving south away from him until she found the perfect spot. From her small pocketbook, she pulled out a black disc about the size of a dessert plate.

She slid her hand into the center of the disc. A faint green light read her signature, and the device began to unfold. It expanded until it was two feet in width and a foot deep. Belle quickly stripped out of her clothing. The jewels made of glamor she dismissed while the dress and shoes went into the disc.

A small flash flame device had the clothing incinerated in under a minute. Once the clothes were ashes, the device reformed to its original size. She stuck it back in the purse and pulled out new clothes to go back into the ball. She had one more piece of business before she could leave.

Encased in a designer black silk side hi-low. Her long blonde swept back into a chignon. Wisp of blonde hair framed her delicate features, making her blue eyes stand out. Bejeweled strappy heels with a silver stiletto heel graced her feet. The last piece of wardrobe was a ten-carat diamond choker.

Peter Luciano

I get what I want and I want Wendi Deveraux. She sings at my sworn enemy's nightclub. It will be all the sweeter taking her from James Bruno.

Wendi Deveraux

I sing to pay my mother's hospital bills, but I hate James Bruno whose club has become my gilded cage. Hope begins to grow when Peter Luciano promises he can open Bruno's cruel grasp.

Belle Night

I'm in love with my boss, Peter Luciano, but he doesn't see me. Now he demands I help his latest conquest get free of a man he's hated for years. How can I remove the jagged pieces of my broken heart?

www.ingramcontent.com/pod-product-compliance
Lightning Source LLC
Chambersburg PA
CBHW010558170726
48285CB00011B/2964